The Dawn of Peace

An Etherya's Earth Prequel

By

REBECCA HEFNER

Cover Design: Authortree, authortree.co
Editor and Proofreader: Bryony Leah, www.bryonyleah.com

Contents

For new and seasoned readers of this series. I always wanted to write a prequel for you—it just took me a few years to get around to it! Enjoy the HEA.

Chapter 1

Six Years after the Awakening

Kilani, daughter of esteemed Slayer council member Pretorius, clenched her teeth as she swung the sword through the air. Her task required extreme concentration since it was imperative she didn't hurt the person at the other end of the weapon. Although her sparring partner was only fourteen years old, she was already fierce with a sword.

"Use your height to your advantage, Miranda," Kilani said, slicing the weapon low by her hip.

"I don't have any height," Miranda gritted, advancing and thrusting the sword toward Kilani's abdomen. "Damn it, I thought I had you."

Kilani held up a hand, halting their skirmish. "You did well, my princess. You only started training weeks ago. Give it time."

Nodding, Miranda ran a hand over her sleek black hair, secured into a tiny ponytail at her nape. "You know, both our fathers would kill us if they knew we were training. We're not playing the appropriate female roles for the austere Slayer kingdom." Her lips formed a cheeky grin.

"I'm not sure you'll ever fit that mold, Miranda, and for that, I am grateful. The War of the Species rages, and it must end before it destroys both tribes."

"I hate that our species have devolved to this point. Vampyres and Slayers existed in peace for centuries before the Awakening."

Cupping her shoulder, Kilani gave a reassuring squeeze. "Hopefully, all will be well again one day, princess. The war will end, Slayers will live without fear, and Vampyres will walk in the sun once more."

"And they can finally stop raiding us for our blood...the vein-sucking jerks."

Kilani cleared her throat. "I think your father would faint if he heard you speak in such a manner."

Miranda's lips twitched. "Then let's keep it between us."

Kenden, Miranda's cousin and commander of the Slayer army, chose that moment to appear, stepping into the clearing from the surrounding woods. "Miranda," he said in his deep baritone, "King Marsias is looking for you. It's time to return to the castle."

"Fine," she sighed, handing her sword to Kilani, "but we made progress today. I'm getting better."

"One day, you'll be a powerful warrior. Hopefully by then, we can talk your father into rescinding the decree that women can't fight in the army."

"I'm proud you would welcome women into the army, Ken," Miranda said, patting him on the shoulder. "And Kilani should be your first recruit. She's amazing with a sword."

"I only agreed to let her train you when I was unavailable," Kenden said, arching a brow. "I don't want you dragged into an untenable situation, Kilani. If your father or King Marsias learn we're training Miranda, there will be hell to pay."

"Understood," Kilani said with a nod. "Father and I have never seen eye to eye on these matters. Misogyny has reared its ugly head in our kingdom now that war is upon us. It's amazing how people revert to their base beliefs, no matter how antiquated, when they are thrust into harrowing situations. I would worry for the state of our kingdom, but I know Miranda will pull us back to the light one day."

"If Father ever lets me take the throne," she muttered. "Every day, he morphs into someone colder—someone I barely recognize. It's chilling to look into his eyes and see the darkness there. I hope he doesn't lose himself in an effort to win the war."

"Your mother's abduction and death at the hands of Deamon King Crimeous destroyed him. His pain clouds his judgment and fuels his anger. We'll do our best to steer him down the right path," Kenden said. "For now, you must go, Miranda."

With a nod, she waved to both of them before heading into the forest and disappearing from sight.

"Marsias is intent on remaining king," Kilani said softly. "I don't see him relinquishing the throne to Miranda for decades, maybe even centuries. It's possible she'll eventually have to wrest it from him by force."

Inhaling a deep breath, Kenden nodded. "I foresee many obstacles in the dark days that lie ahead. The Vampyre army is vast, and with their self-healing abilities, we lose twice as many men as they do in each battle."

"Which is why women should be allowed to join the army," she said, chin lifting.

"Yes." Kenden kicked the ground with the toe of his boot. "But Marsias will never allow it, nor will the council. Your father is one of the most vocal supporters of an all-male army."

"My father is an old man who is only alive because of our cursed immortality. I swear, the goddess should've bestowed us with finite lives for people like him."

Kenden's features softened. "I'm sorry your relationship with him is so strained. I miss my family terribly since they were killed in the Awakening and have no idea what it's like not to love those most closely related to you by blood."

Pondering, Kilani pursed her lips. Seconds passed before she said, "You just learn to live without love. Some things are more important."

He flashed a compassionate smile beneath his straight nose and mop of brown hair. "You will find a great love one day. Of that, I have no doubt."

"Okay," she said, waving her hand. "Go home to Leticia. I don't have time for frivolous discussions."

"Leticia and I ended things," he said, lifting his shoulder. "I'm just too busy with the troops and the war. I hope she finds someone who can give her what I can't."

"I'm sorry to hear that. If we're not careful, my father and King Marsias will try to push us together as they always do when we're both single. Of course, trying to kiss you would be like kissing my brother, although I do like you a tad more." She grinned and held her thumb and index finger an inch apart.

"I'll take that as a compliment...I think." He squinted. "Speaking of your brother, I hear your father is preparing him to take his spot on the council when he retires."

"He tells Drakor that to appease him, but Father will never give up his seat."

"It should be your seat since you are firstborn."

"Council members have always been men. Hopefully, Miranda will change things when she becomes queen. Having the blood of King Valktor makes her the one true heir. Marsias is just a placeholder."

"A powerful placeholder," Kenden said. "His desire to avenge Queen Rina is vast. Since the prophecy states that someone with Valktor's blood will kill the Deamon Lord Crimeous, and Miranda is Valktor's only living descendant, I feel he will want her to bear a male heir."

Scoffing, she fisted her hands on her hips. "Of course. Because a *female* could never kill Crimeous. Rubbish." She gave a *pfft* and felt her cheeks inflame with anger.

"You are ahead of your time, Kilani. The kingdom is not ready for you, nor will they be ready when it's Miranda's time to assume power. The transition must be handled with care."

"I'll offer my help, although Father likes to relegate me to societal duties. He has no idea you trained me to fight."

Kenden's eyebrows lifted. "Honestly, I was floored when you asked me to train you after the Awakening, but I see the value in teaching those who want to learn. If I have that foresight, I trust others can acquire it too."

"We'll see," she muttered, rubbing her arm. "In the meantime, I should get going. Father is hosting a fundraising dinner for Marsias so he can dazzle the aristocrats into funneling more money into the war. The fight against the Vampyres is costly, especially now since we have to line the compound walls with armed soldiers to protect us from the raids."

"That it is. I assume you organized the fete?"

She nodded. "It's my duty to organize all social functions since Mother died. I hate it with a passion, but it is easier to comply than fight with Father." Her eyes narrowed. "I don't remember getting an RSVP from you."

"I have a night training."

"Lucky you." Sighing, she ran her hand through the blond hair that fell slightly past her shoulders. "Well then, let me get to it. I'd much rather meet you at the sparring field under the moon."

"It will happen one day, Kilani," he said with an encouraging squeeze of her shoulder.

"Let's win the war, and then we can drag the kingdom into modernity."

"From your lips to the goddess's ears."

His eyebrow arched. "We renounced the goddess when she withdrew her protection from our people."

Kilani shrugged. "She cursed the Vampyres to darkness, causing their skin to burn if they even step into the sun. Perhaps she did her best to punish both species equally."

"Perhaps."

"On that uplifting little note, I'm off," she said, raising a hand and giving a salute. "See ya."

Kenden's goodbye followed her through the woods as her boots crunched the fallen leaves and branches. Eventually, she reached the clearing that bordered her father's home and trailed across the long meadow.

Once inside, she snuck through the back door, ensuring none of the servants observed her in her black sparring gear. After showering, she pulled the long, flowing red gown from her closet, wrinkling her nose in distaste. God, she hated formal dresses. Dragging it over her head, she smoothed the fabric before applying a bare smattering of makeup. After pulling her hair into a functional yet elegant bun, Kilani headed downstairs to ensure everything was prepared for the fundraiser she was dreading with every cell in her body.

Chapter 2

F our hours later, Kilani lifted her wineglass to her lips, sipping the dark red liquid as she tried not to die of boredom. One of the aristocratic Slayers she'd known for decades was chatting her ear off as they sat at the expansive table in the mansion's ornate dining room. She was pretty sure her father had switched the place seating cards so her seat was next to Friedan's. Pretorius thought he was wily, but Kilani was all too familiar with his futile and transparent matchmaking attempts.

"Kilani," Friedan asked, "did I lose you?"

"No, just enjoying the wine," was her curt reply. "I think I need to take a walk before the dancing begins. Please excuse me." Tossing back the wine, she set the glass on the table and rose, craving fresh air.

Once outside, she rested her hands on the cool stone of the balcony rail, gazing up at the full moon as she shivered in the crisp nighttime air. Vampyres were known to raid Uteria during the full moon since it offered additional light for their conquests. But they'd raided the compound the previous month, thereby decreasing the chances they would attack again so soon. Vampyre King Sathan was known to keep Slayer prisoners alive in his dungeon so he could extract every drop of blood from their veins and bank it for his people.

"Blood-sucking bastards," she muttered, her breath forming a puff in the chilly air. "I'm so tired of this fucking war."

"I hoped you would enjoy talking to Friedan tonight," her father's deep voice called behind her, "but instead, you stand out here talking to yourself. You will never find a husband this way, Kilani."

Closing her eyes, she inhaled a deep breath, silently instructing herself to remain calm. The last thing she needed was another blowout with her father.

"I have no wish to get married or find a mate," she said, lifting her lids. Her gaze bore into his, showing her fortitude. "I wish to be a solider, Father. Once Miranda is old enough to take the throne, I will pledge my skills to the kingdom and fight to protect it."

Pretorius scoffed. "It will never happen. You dream of a future that will never be. I implore you to dismiss these thoughts and find a suitable mate."

Sighing, she shook her head. "I can't have this argument with you again, Father. Let's just agree to disagree, shall we?" Wishing to change the subject, she gestured toward the brightly lit home. "The fundraiser is going well."

"It is." Glancing down, his eyebrows drew together before he lifted his gaze to hers. "I won't have a daughter who defies me, Kilani. If you do not wish to live by my rules, I have no choice but to petition King Marsias for banishment."

Kilani's heartbeat began to thrum in her chest. Surely, he wasn't serious? They had disagreed for centuries, but she at least thought he cared for her, even if he didn't love her as he did her brother and deceased mother.

"Father, if you banish me to Restia, there will be no one here to perform Mother's duties. I thought you at least needed me to fill that role."

"Not to Restia," he said, his tone firm. "I will petition to ban you from the Slayer kingdom. If you wish to be so progressive, perhaps you should cross the ether and live with the humans. Maybe that will teach you our societal rules aren't the prison sentence you insist they are."

Fear coursed through her at the thought of leaving the only home she'd ever known, along with a healthy dose of anger. "You would banish me because we disagree? Because I'm a woman who wants to *choose* her own fate? That's absurd!"

"It's necessary!" he said, slicing a hand through the air. "I won't continue to live with the embarrassment of having a daughter who refuses to adhere to societal rules that have existed for centuries."

"Which means they're antiquated and need to change!" she demanded, exasperated. "Whether you like it or not, change will come to this kingdom. Miranda *will* become queen one day, and it's possible that with her leadership, the War of the Species will also end."

"Slayers and Vampyres will never live in peace again," he said, dismissing her statements as if they were insignificant. "You clutch onto a life and dreams that will never be." Lifting his finger, he cocked an eyebrow. "This is your last warning, Kilani. Find a husband by the next harvest, or I will begin banishment proceedings."

Clenching her fists, Kilani struggled not to punch him in his straight, austere nose. "You understand I will never accept this," she murmured.

"Then you have *chosen* your own fate," he said, using her previous words against her. "I hope it's worth it."

"You bastard!" she hissed, jabbing her finger in his face. "You have never treated me as an equal part of this family—"

"Because you don't do your part," he interjected. "You have a role to fill. If you cannot do it, I have no use for you."

Pain sliced through every pore of her skin, the words searing as if she'd been doused in acid. As emotion swirled deep in her gut, her ears perked, and she gasped before glancing toward the far end of the meadow.

Recognition lit in her father's eyes before he pivoted, staring out across the dark field.

Suddenly, cries of war echoed across the fog-ridden meadow, and Kilani's eyes widened.

"Go inside and inform the guests the Vampyres are raiding."

"Kilani—"

"Go," she said, facing him with disgust. "I have a sword stashed in the garden shed. I will arm myself and do my best to fight them off. Gather everyone in the basement and lock it behind you. Do you hear me?"

Something sparked in his dark orbs as he gazed at her, and Kilani had the strange thought this would be the last time she ever saw her father.

"Go!" she yelled.

His throat bobbed in the moonlight before he pivoted and scurried inside.

Straightening her spine, Kilani prepared for battle. Her faith in Kenden was firm, and she knew he would arrive soon with troops. In the meantime, she would put her training to good use.

Stalking to the shed, she yanked open the door and strode to the sword. Glancing at the small shearers that hung on the wall, she stuck those in the belt at the waist of her flowing dress. And then she marched outside, sword in hand, ready to fight the Vampyres.

Chapter 3

Alrec, son of Vampyre soldier Jakar, crested the hill that overlooked the massive Slayer mansion. Lights burned brightly inside as Slayer aristocrats held the fundraiser to finance the War of the Species.

"The troops are ready to advance, sir," Takel's deep baritone droned beside him. He was an excellent warrior, and Alrec was thankful to have him as his first-in-command.

"Good," Alrec said, scanning the open field and the mansion beyond. "I'm frustrated we're here again so soon, but King Marsias's suicide decree leaves us no choice." The stubborn ruler had commanded any Slayer who was abducted to end his life rather than survive in the dungeon and become food for Vampyres. Ten of the Slayer men abducted in the last raid had somehow secured a toothpick—most likely carelessly tossed on the floor by one of the Vampyre dungeon guards—and they'd used it to fulfill King Marsias's decree.

Sighing, Alrec ran a hand over his face. So much death in the endless war the Vampyres fought with the Slayers. How long could they go on like this?

"Alrec?" Takel asked.

Dragging himself out of the morose thoughts, he pulled the sword from the hilt on his waist and held it high. "Secure ten Slayer men and then retreat," he called to his battalion. "I have no wish to drag out this raid."

The men chimed a united, "Yes, sir!" behind him before he shook his sword and yelled, "Charge!"

Adrenaline rushed through his veins as he surged down the hill, crossing the meadow as his boots crunched the grass below. His battalion of twenty Vampyres followed close behind, ready to fulfill their duty.

Suddenly, a flash of golden hair caught his eye under the silver moonlight, and Alrec's breath lodged in his throat. A Slayer woman stood tall, sword in hand, as her kinsmen scurried behind her, fleeing like ants toward the safety of the bunkers below the home.

"I will confront the female!" Alrec yelled to his men, indicating they should continue past him toward the mansion. "Seize the Slayer men and retreat quickly!"

The soldiers charged forward, scurrying toward the back entrance of the mansion as Alrec approached the woman. As he drew near, he noticed the flowing red gown clinging to her frame as she lifted the sword. Both hands clenched the hilt, her azure eyes glowing under the darkened sky, and Alrec felt his heart clank in his chest.

She was *magnificent.*

Regaining his wits, he trudged toward her, hoping she would recognize the futility of fighting him. As he drew closer, their height and weight discrepancy became clear. He towered over her by at least a foot, and his muscled body outweighed her by several stone.

"Lower your sword, little one," he called, surprised by the protective swell in his voice. "I have no wish to harm you."

"Little one, my ass," she responded, teeth clenched as she lifted the sword higher. "I'll be damned if you abduct my people without putting up a fight."

Halting when he was close enough to strike, he planted his feet and slowly lifted his hand, showing her his palm. "I don't want to fight you. I can kill you in seconds. Is that really what you wish?"

Midnight blue eyes roved over his features. "I would rather die a noble death defending my fellow Slayers than let you abduct us without a fight." Aiming the tip of her sword toward him, she crouched. "Come on, *Vampyre*," she sneered, her tone full of malice. "Let's see how tough you are when you're against a Slayer with the temerity to fight back!" She charged until he had no choice but to defend himself.

The steel of their blades crashed together, the clanking sound ominous against the cries and shrills of war in the background. The Slayer was quick, her movements deft, and a surge of elation jolted down his spine. Alrec relished being a warrior, and there was nothing more thrilling than a worthy opponent.

He thrust his sword through the air, connecting with hers every few seconds before retreating and trying a different angle. The vexing woman seemed to anticipate his every move, and he realized her training was vast.

"Who trained you?" he gritted, pressing his sword to hers as the weapons crossed between their bodies. "You are exceptional."

"Kenden trained me himself, you blood-sucking bastard," she cried before drawing back and rotating. Heaving her sword, she lodged it in his shoulder, causing a surge of pain before he grasped it with his large hand and yanked it from his skin.

"Well done," he mocked, squeezing the blade as she gaped up at him, the small sliver of fear in her stunning irises both pleasing and disconcerting. Blood dripped from his hand where he clutched the blade—and his shoulder where she'd stabbed him—but his self-healing abilities would quickly repair the wounds. Pain rushed through his body as he tossed her sword to the ground. Although he would self-heal, he still felt pain.

The woman gasped, nostrils flaring as she gazed up at him.

"You've lost possession of your weapon," he said, gesturing with his head toward her sword, which now sat several feet away on the soft grass. "Our skirmish is over—"

The blasted woman drew something from her belt that flashed in the moonlight before she thrust it into his abdomen. Sucking in a breath, Alrec realized she'd stabbed him with some sort of pruning shears.

"Good grief, woman!" he bellowed, grasping the handle and dislodging the sharp metal from his body. "Is it your objective to anger me until I kill you? You know your meager weapons will only hurt and my wounds will heal quickly. Only an eight-shooter or a poison-tipped blade can kill me, and you seem to have neither."

"I'll fight you with my bare hands," she cried, balling her fists.

Pain sluiced through his body as he simultaneously fought the urge to laugh and knock the Slayer unconscious. She was a piece of work indeed. Never had he met a woman with her grit and determination.

"We have ten Slayers!" Takel's voice chimed from across the meadow. "Should we retreat?"

"Yes," Alrec confirmed, backing away from the Slayer as she stood crouched in her fighting stance. Overcome with admiration for her, he decided to let her live.

"What is your name?" he asked, backing toward the far-off hill, needing to know before he retreated.

"Kilani, daughter of Pretorius, and you'll regret the day you abducted my kinsmen, Vampyre."

"No doubt," he murmured, rubbing the laceration on his abdomen as he studied her. "We don't wish to abduct your people. Tell Marsias to end the suicide decree. Next time, I won't be so nice, little one. Remember that when you speak to your king." Sparing her one last glance, he pivoted and ran across the field to join his men.

Strangely, the Slayer woman's stunning image remained in his mind long after the new prisoners had been secured in the dungeon. Eventually, after several nights of dreaming about her, Alrec accepted his fierce little warrior would always have permanent residence in the part of his brain it seemed couldn't let her go.

Chapter 4

Kilani's heart pounded as she digested the fact the hulking Vampyre had let her live. Although she'd put up a good fight, he could've easily overpowered her. Mulling over his actions, she turned to face the mansion. Kenden's soldiers were now on the scene, and he jogged toward her, concern lacing his features.

"Are you okay?" he asked, breathless as he approached and rested a hand on her shoulder.

"Yes. I fought the battalion leader, but he let me live." Brushing dirt off her arm, she scowled. "Bastard. Now I'm indebted to a Vampyre." Glancing toward the house, Kilani observed the chaos as soldiers scrambled and Slayers cried over the men who'd been abducted. "It's never going to end, is it?" she asked softly.

"One day," Kenden murmured. "For now, we should get you to the infirmary just in case."

"I'm fine," she said, backing away. Staring at the cold stones of the mansion, a sense of finality washed over her. "I have no place in this kingdom, Ken. I don't want to marry for duty, and Marsias won't allow women in the army. I'm fighting for a kingdom that doesn't want me."

"Things will change, Kilani—"

"When?" she cried, lifting her hands. "Once our men are dead and the Vampyres have depleted their only food rations? In the meantime, will I continue to live a miserable life in a world where my father is intent on banishment?"

Kenden's eyebrows drew together. "He threatened to banish you?"

Kilani nodded, contemplative under the dark sky as a plan formed in her rapidly buzzing brain. "I won't let him dictate my life, Ken."

Chestnut irises darted over her. "What do you want to do?"

Swallowing thickly, she backed toward the darkness of the nearby forest. "Tell them I was killed by the Vampyres, trying to defend our people."

"Kilani," he said, a soft plea in his voice as she inched toward the woods. "You don't have to do this..."

"I'm making a choice. Perhaps the only one I have left."

Sighing, Kenden rubbed his forehead. "I can't let you—"

"Tell Miranda I said goodbye," she said, her voice raspy with emotion. "She has the power to save us all. She will always have my support."

Kenden's expression was soulful and sad under the twinkling stars. "There is an abandoned cabin on the outskirts of the Portal of Mithos, near the foothills of the Strok Mountains. It's secluded, and I doubt anyone would find you unless they knew to look. I used to go hunting nearby with my father before he was slain at the Awakening."

"Who built it?" she asked, curious as she edged deeper into the woods.

"I don't know. It was there long before we hunted but has been abandoned for decades, maybe even centuries. It sits near a lake where fish are abundant."

"Thank you." Barely able to speak since her throat was so tight, she lifted her hand and waved. "Until I see you again, Ken. Thank you for letting me go."

"Goodbye, Kilani," he said with a small salute. "May I see you again when the world is ready for you."

With one last glance at his soulful expression, Kilani memorized her friend's features, hoping the image would comfort her in the life of solitude she was embarking upon. And then she turned and ran deep into the woods, past the walls of the compound, to an eternity where she would be alone but finally able to control her own destiny.

Chapter 5

Five years later

Alrec grunted, slicing his sword through the air as he fought the Deamon. This particular cluster of Deamons who lived at the base of the Strok Mountains were vicious, and Alrec's battalion had been tracking them for some time. Not only had they attacked a Vampyre unit stationed outside Astaria's wall several weeks ago, but they had also raided the Slayer compound of Uteria the previous week.

Alrec's battalion had been assigned to track down the bastards and eradicate them before they could cause more harm—to Vampyres or Slayers. After all, Slayers were their food, and they needed to remain alive.

And he didn't want any harm to befall his golden-haired Slayer warrior.

Yes, somewhere along the way, through sweat-soaked dreams and hazy visions, she'd become *his* Slayer. Alrec had long since realized the futility of trying to rid her from his mind. She lived there rent-free and most likely always would.

It was quite a cluster since Vampyres and Slayers were locked in a war neither side was able to win and romantic love between species was forbidden. Different species couldn't bear children, and Etherya decreed the species remain separate eons ago. Not to mention Alrec's desire for the Slayer he hadn't seen in five long years was unwanted. He'd prayed to the goddess countless times to rid the woman from his mind, but Alrec was also practical. Erasing the image of her gorgeous face was a futile endeavor, and he was a man who didn't waste time.

So, he carried on, eventually becoming used to the woman's stunning features inhabiting every crevice of his brain.

The Deamon landed a powerful blow to his side, dragging Alrec back to the battle. Thrusting his sword high, he fought the Deamon, edging him closer to the riverbank as the Vampyre battalion fought behind him. Their shouts and cries of war grew softer as Alrec advanced, hoping his men were aware of his location.

Suddenly, the Deamon tossed his sword to the ground and pulled a weapon from his belt. Gasping, Alrec realized it was a mini eight-shooter. The weapon had been developed by the powerful Slayer commander, Kenden, and was one of the few devices capable of killing self-healing Vampyres. If fired, it would simultaneously deploy eight bullets into a Vampyre's eight-chambered heart, killing him on contact.

"You don't want to do this," Alrec said, holding up his hands as he clutched the sword tight in one fist. Searching his surroundings, he looked for high ground where he could retreat and regroup. "I am the battalion leader, and my men won't show mercy if you kill me."

"I don't care, Vampyre!" the Deamon spat. "You are all expendable to us."

Thinking quickly, Alrec decided he would run toward the river and dive in. The current was strong, and he would probably be carried several miles, but he was a competent survivalist and would be able to navigate back home to Astaria eventually. Frustration curled in his gut that he saw no angle to strike the Deamon, but Alrec liked living and was smart enough to know his sword and strength were no match for a direct blow from an eight-shooter. Inhaling a deep breath, he filled his lungs with oxygen and sprinted toward the river.

The Deamon gasped, turning and firing at the same moment Alrec dove into the cold, rushing water. The last thing he heard was a small explosion, followed by a powerful burst of pain in his side. Then he became submerged, and all he saw was darkness.

Takel scanned the horizon beyond the river, frustrated his men hadn't yet found Alrec. After they'd defeated the Deamons and the few left alive scattered in retreat, they spent hours searching for their missing battalion leader. Unfortunately, they had no results and the sun would soon rise, burning them all to death.

"Takel," a deep voice chimed as a firm hand cupped his shoulder, "we have to head back to camp. We can send a battalion to search for Alrec tomorrow night. We won't rest until we find him."

Sighing, Takel nodded. "You're right, Draylock. I'm worried he was injured with a poison-tipped blade or struck by an eight-shooter. I hope we find him alive."

"We'll do our best. For now, our men need rest, and dawn is near."

Resigned to return to look for his friend, Takel pivoted from the river and led the battalion back to their base.

Chapter 6

Kilani exited the cabin, lifting her face to the sky and stretching as the faint sounds of birds chirping pulsed through the air. She'd always loved dawn. Something about it was refreshing, reminding the soul it had another day to get things right. Inhaling the fresh air, she reveled in the crisp tingle in her nose before clutching the spear at her side and trailing to the river.

In the five years she'd inhabited the cabin, it had become her home. When she discovered it, the wood and stone that comprised the foundation were overgrown with brush. The inside had a large bed with pillows and a mattress filled with goose feathers. A handmade sofa and two chairs comprised the only other furniture, and as she'd inspected the abandoned home, curiosity ran rampant.

Running her fingers over the sofa, she'd imagined it had been fashioned for a child or spouse by someone who loved them. Where had they gone? Judging by the sticky cobwebs and thick layer of dust, the home had been abandoned for some time. Never one to shy away from good fortune, Kilani had cleaned and polished the interior, determined to make the place feel like home, for it was the only home she would know until she could return to the Slayer kingdom, and she realized she might not feel safe enough to do that for centuries.

So, she toiled in her new home until it was pristine and learned how to fish. After constructing a fishing pole from a tree branch and some twine she'd found in the closet, she realized waiting patiently for fish to bite the bait wasn't her forte. Patience had never been her strong suit after all. Instead, she fashioned a spear from a stronger branch and taught herself to spear the fish. After some practice, she became quite good at it and now lived on a diet of fish and vegetables she grew in the garden. Some days, she would long for the rich food she'd become accustomed to as a Slayer aristocrat before she remembered food came with a hefty side of misogyny and repression. Upon those cheery thoughts, she would scowl and chew the damn fish, savoring every bite.

It was a solitary life, although she wasn't lonely. Kilani had been lonelier stuck in a life where she had no choice. Here, on her small patch of Etherya's Earth, she could grow into someone stronger. Someone who could possibly return to the Slayer kingdom sometime in the future when Miranda had fulfilled the prophecy and saved them all.

"Hell," Kilani muttered to herself as she traipsed toward the river, "you might be patient after all. Maybe living in the woods has worked miracles."

Approaching the riverbank, she noticed the clouds turn from gray to yellow and knew the sun would soon rise. The fish were always plentiful at dawn, and she gazed into the murky water, ready to catch her breakfast.

Something flashed out of the corner of her eye, and Kilani held her gasp, not wanting to make a sound if danger was near. Gripping her spear, she inched toward the sparkle in the distance. Approaching, a soft cry exited her lips as the image became clearer. The sparkling object was a metal button on a weaponry belt...and it was attached to a very large, very injured Vampyre. Blood trickled from eight small wounds on the side of his chest, and he was immobile except for the slight pulsing of the vein in his neck. Leaning down, Kilani jutted the blunt tip of the spear against his shoulder, confirming he was unconscious.

Grasping his stubbled chin, she turned his face, already knowing he was a Vampyre because of his huge frame but wanting to confirm he had fangs to satisfy her assumption. Glancing at his features, she inhaled a deep breath.

The Vampyre was the man who had spared her life five years ago in the raid at her father's home.

Releasing his chin, Kilani straightened and stared at the sky. As soon as the sun rose, it would burn his body to a crisp. Clenching her jaw, she knew what she had to do. Although she hated Vampyres, she also had an inherent sense of honor, and this man had spared her life once before. Now, it was time to return the favor.

Pivoting, she jogged to the cabin and grabbed the pallet she used to haul wood for the fireplace. After dragging it back to the river, she grunted and grumbled as she maneuvered the Vampyre's injured body atop the slats. Gripping the rope, she hauled the massive Vampyre back to her cabin, ensuring he was inside before the sun rose.

Needing to inspect his wounds, she removed his clothes and shoved him into the bed, covering him with the sheet before she gave in to her curiosity and inspected his more...*intimate* anatomy. After securing his wrists and ankles to each bedpost with her strongest ropes, she stood at the foot of the bed and gazed upon his unconscious frame, wondering how in the hell she'd ended up with a half-dead Vampyre in her bed.

Chapter 7

Alrec climbed toward consciousness, pain pulsing at the side of his chest. Reaching for the wound, he grunted, frustrated his arms wouldn't work. Struggling to open his eyes, he focused all his energy on lifting his eyelids, which seemed fused together. Eventually, they fluttered, and Alrec slowly lifted them, squinting at the dim light that eased through.

Adrenaline surged through his frame as he realized he was naked in what appeared to be a warm bed. Gazing down, he noticed the sheet covering his torso and legs and the ropes that secured each ankle to a bedpost. Tugging his arms, he grunted when he could barely move them. Sensing a presence at the foot of the bed, he glanced down and tried to focus.

A woman stepped forward, and the first thing Alrec noticed was her hair. The golden crown of hair he'd seen in his dreams for five long years, followed by her pert nose, full red lips, and eyes the color of the blue moss that grew atop the lake beside his childhood home at Astaria.

Widening his eyes, he whispered, "It's *you*."

She arched one of those golden eyebrows, her expression sardonic as she gazed at him above her crossed arms.

"Yes," she said with a nod. "I was wondering if you'd remember me. I remembered you when I found you minutes from death by the riverbank. The mercy you showed me years ago is the only reason you're alive."

Alrec blinked several times as he processed everything he knew about his current situation. He'd been fighting the Deamons when one of the bastards cornered him by the riverbank. Alrec had jumped into the river to avoid his eight-shooter blast...and then all had gone dark.

"Am I...?" Glancing down at his wound, which was covered by a white bandage, he cleared his throat. "Am I in the Passage?"

She scoffed and shook her head. "No such luck, buddy. You're stuck here in paradise with me. Who knew it resided between the Deamon Caves and the Strok Mountains? Surprise." She held up her hands and waved them in a mock cheer.

"Okay..." he said, struggling to understand why the Slayer had saved him. "You've been nursing me? Why haven't I self-healed?"

Striding forward, she neared his side and gently ran her fingers over his bandage, causing Alrec to shiver. The sight of her slender hand trailing over his body jump-started his pulse, and his heartbeat thudded inside his injured chest.

"I don't know," she murmured, absently staring at the bandage. "I don't have the proper tools here to test the poison in the bullets that were lodged in your chest. But I removed them, and they were laced with something quite nasty. Eight-shooters with poison-tipped bullets are known to kill a Vampyre in seconds. Even though the bullets didn't make it to your heart, I think they were close enough to circulate the poison throughout your side and chest. You're slowly healing, but it will take time."

Alrec's eyebrows drew together. "Fucking Crimeous. He continues to create deadlier poisons as the conflict worsens. It makes him formidable, which is the last thing we need."

She smirked. "Since you're already in a deadly war with the Slayers."

"Yes," he muttered, annoyance growing with each minute he remained restrained. "Fighting the Deamon King and the Slayers requires extensive time and effort. This is why I was here with my battalion. We were surveilling the Deamon outpost to gather intel. It's imperative we learn their weaknesses."

The woman flattened her lips, appearing smug as he lay in the bed.

"I'm not sure what the shit-eating grin is for, but it would be nice if you would untie me," he said, pulling at the restraints.

Leaning down, the tips of her hair brushed his chest as her warm breath floated across his face. "I know one of their weaknesses," she almost whispered, "and there's no way in hell I'm untying you."

Anger surged down his spine along with a hefty dose of arousal at the woman's scent. It was laced with hints of evergreen and mint as fresh as the wind on a warm spring night. Struggling to keep the desire at bay, he clenched his teeth.

"Do you really think I'm going to hurt the woman who saved me?"

She glanced at the ceiling, pondering. Finally, she shrugged and straightened. "Debatable." Gazing down, her eyes focused on the rather large tenting of the sheet at the juncture of his thighs. Alrec remained still, unwilling to squirm under her scrutiny. "Although, judging by your...*reaction,* you seem more like a lover than a fighter."

"Kilani," he said softly, pleased when she gasped and lifted her eyes to his. "Yes, I remember your name. I couldn't forget the name of such a magnificent warrior." *Or such a beautiful woman.* Holding his tongue, he allowed that sentiment to remain unsaid. "I give you my word I won't hurt you. And if you're willing to share any intel you've gathered on the Deamons, I would be forever grateful."

Tilting her head, she studied him as if he were a bug under a microscope. Finally, she lifted a finger and spoke in a firm tone. "The word of a Vampyre means nothing to me. And I have no wish to help a soldier I met when he was previously raiding my people for their blood. Be careful you don't anger me," she said, reaching for the glass full of murky liquid on the nightstand. "I still might decide to kill you." Touching the rim of the glass to his lips, she whispered in an ominous tone, "Drink up."

Alrec struggled before she slid her fingers through his hair and yanked, holding his head in place and all but pouring the liquid down his throat.

"By the goddess, that's awful!" he exclaimed, coughing and sputtering as he swallowed. "Is it poison?"

"Relax," she muttered, rolling her eyes. "It's an herbal concoction I made that will help you heal...and help you sleep. I have things to do around here and can't entertain an injured Vampyre all day. Sweet dreams." Rapidly blinking, she stood and gave a jeering wave. "See you on the other side."

Alrec opened his mouth to tell her he didn't appreciate the mocking tone...except speaking suddenly felt like a massive effort. Lowering his lids, he felt his head loll to the side...and then he fell down the hole of darkness once again.

Chapter 8

The next time Alrec opened his eyes, he was immediately drawn to the muted curses and whimpers of frustration uttered by the Slayer as she stood over the counter. Struggling to focus in the dim light, he wondered what was causing her pain.

"Kilani?" he called, the words hoarse since his throat was as dry as sandpaper. "Are you hurt?"

Those midnight blue eyes snapped to his as she stood behind the small island counter. It was made of wood, and Alrec found himself wondering if she'd fashioned it herself. How long had she been living alone in the woods? Was she hiding from something or someone?

"I'm fine," she muttered, squeezing her wrist so a small trickle of blood fell into the glass below. "You have to eat, don't you?"

Remaining silent, Alrec admitted she was right. A Vampyre needed Slayer blood every three days to survive. Although they ate food for pleasure, the goddess had made the species interdependent so they would be tethered together for eternity. Slayers offered their blood for sustenance, and Vampyres protected them in return—until the Awakening, when it had all gone horribly wrong.

Kilani poured approximately one ounce of blood into the glass before rubbing salve over the small wound on her wrist and applying a bandage. Grabbing the glass, she sauntered over, the sway of her hips in her cream-colored pants mesmerizing.

"Here," she said softly, sitting on the side of the bed. "I won't force it down like the tea." Her lips twitched as she lifted the cup to his lips. "I think you'll like this better anyway."

Alrec eyed her warily as he drank, immediately becoming consumed with the taste of her blood on his tongue. It was thick and quite rich, indicating she came from a pristine Slayer bloodline.

"You're an aristocrat," he said after swallowing.

"Yes." Gazing down at the empty glass, her expression grew morose. "I was until I realized being a female aristocrat in our kingdom was more a prison than a privilege. I left the night you attacked...and never looked back."

Alrec's eyes roved over her features, curiosity rampant as he longed to ask more questions. Unsure which to ask first, he decided it was best to let her lead. Clearing his throat, he said softly, "I would like to know your story, Kilani."

Her gaze lifted to his, surprise crossing those stunning features. "You would?"

"Yes." Grinning, he tilted his head on the pillow. "Is that such a strange request of the woman who saved me?"

Sighing, she rubbed her arm and stared absently toward the kitchen. "I don't know. I'm not used to men asking for my story. They usually just tell me who I'm supposed to be. Except for Kenden. He was one of a kind."

A strange spurt of jealously flared in his chest. Kenden was the powerful Slayer commander who had built a competent army after the Awakening. It was quite a feat considering Slayers weren't built for war like Vampyres. Narrowing his eyes, Alrec realized he didn't relish the little Slayer's wistful smile. Had they been lovers?

"Oh, no," she said, shaking her head, and Alrec realized he'd blurted the question aloud. "Ken was like my brother and helped lead me here. He's the only person in the immortal world who knows I'm still alive except for you,"—she arched a brow—"and I am grateful he keeps my secret."

"Why do you exile yourself from your people?"

Sighing, she ran a hand through her silken hair. "They're not ready for me yet. I might go back one day. Once Miranda has taken the throne, fulfilled the prophecy, and can foster positive change in our kingdom. Until then, I choose to remain here." Lifting her eyes to his, she murmured, "It isn't much, but it's my choice, and that's enough."

Alrec longed to hear more—to ask her why she didn't have choices in her kingdom and if she ever wished for companionship. Instead, he stayed silent, his eyes locked on her lithe frame as she trailed to the kitchen and washed the glass.

"Do you get your water from the river?" he asked, noting several full basins lining the countertop.

"Sometimes," she said with a shrug as she dried the glass. "And there's a lake nearby too. The house had some old blankets and curtains when I arrived that I made into clothes." Setting the glass in the drying rack, she drew her hand over her shirt and pants. "They're not the fancy silks I wore at Uteria, but they're comfortable."

She toiled in the kitchen, gathering medical supplies before returning to sit at his side. After setting the supplies on the bedside table, she peeled away the bandage covering his wounds, her face a mask of concentration.

"So strange..." she said, examining his wounds. "I've never heard of a Vampyre taking so long to heal. That poison really got under your skin. Literally."

Picking up a wet cloth, she began to gently clean his wounds, her motions methodical and tender. Her honeyed evergreen scent overwhelmed him, and he looked away, understanding he wouldn't be able to control his body's reaction to her. Whether he liked it or not, he was extremely attracted to the little Slayer.

Thick muscles tensed underneath his skin the longer she tended to him, blood coursing through each vein as if they might explode. Closing his eyes, Alrec felt his shaft thicken and pulse, the sensitive skin growing taut, and he ached for release. Kilani's breathing grew shallow, permeating the quiet room, and he opened his eyes to observe the pounding vein in her neck. Her cheeks now carried a rosy blush, and Alrec was relieved the attraction was mutual.

"Do you want to talk about that?" she asked, glancing toward his massive erection now tenting the covers.

Breathing a laugh, Alrec looked to the ceiling and sighed. "There's not much a man can do when a beautiful woman is touching him. Much less when he's restrained." Tugging at the ropes, he latched onto her gaze. "You could untie me, and we could talk about it."

Full lips curved as she finished her ministrations and began to secure a bandage over his wounds. "Good try, but I've been celibate for a long time. Not sure I'm ready to dive back into that rat's nest. Especially with a Vampyre whose name I don't know. Surely, that's blasphemous for a Slayer female, no?" Her eyes glowed with amusement.

"Alrec," was his soft reply as he noted her shiver at the deep tone of his voice. "My name is Alrec. There is one objection you can remove from your list."

"Alrec," she said, gently patting the bandage to ensure it was secure. "A warrior's name."

He nodded against the pillow. "I'm not an aristocrat like you. My father was a soldier, and his father before him. Both were killed in the Awakening along with the rest of my family."

Compassion swamped her features. "And you survived?"

"I was a new recruit and had been stationed at Valeria to receive the barrels from the blood-banking. The assignment saved my life but took everyone I loved. Now, I aspire to be the best soldier I can to avenge them."

Sadness entered her eyes. "So you hate Slayers as much as I hate Vampyres. So much hatred..." The words trailed off as she glanced away and smoothed a hand over her hair. "We have so much vitriol to overcome. I worry we're doomed."

"I don't hate you, Kilani," he said, his tone soothing. "And perhaps that's a good start. I don't have it in me to hate the Slayer who saved my life."

Glancing at him out of the corner of her eye, she pursed her lips. "Well, I hate you. You saved my life and indebted me to a Vampyre. I'll never forgive you." Mirth sparkled in her eyes as she stood, indicating her teasing. "But honor won't allow me to let you die, so we're stuck with each other...at least until you're well. Then I'll send you back to Astaria, and we can go back to hating each other."

Alrec frowned at the thought of never seeing her again. How strange that his heartbeat quickened at the idea. Although it defied logic, he felt a connection to the Slayer who'd saved his life. Her image had been emblazoned in his brain since he met her on the battlefield years ago. Now that he'd experienced her honor, inhaled her intoxicating scent, and been surrounded by her beauty, he couldn't imagine hating her. But by the goddess, he could imagine loving her...and stroking her golden bronze skin as she writhed in pleasure and moaned his name.

The musings made zero sense, but they persisted nonetheless.

Unable to process them, he leaned his temple on his bicep, staring into her eyes in the hopes she would see his genuineness. "I have no desire to hate you, Kilani. Perhaps we'll even become friends. It would be a positive step toward realigning the species."

Scoffing, she rolled her eyes and trailed back toward the kitchen. "Friends," she muttered, washing her hands in one of the basins. "As if I would ever be friends with a Vampyre."

Alrec was disheartened by her words until she glanced over her shoulder and flashed a slight grin. Elation welled in his chest, and he vowed to earn her friendship in the days ahead. It wouldn't come easily, but somehow, Alrec had never looked forward to anything more in his life.

Chapter 9

A lrec awoke to the distinct feel of something sharp pricking his neck. His eyes roved south, trying to determine the threat level. Kilani stood hunched over the bed, pressing a knife into his skin as she assessed him.

"If this is your idea of foreplay, I think I misjudged you, Kilani."

She shot him a droll look. "Funny. Here's the deal: I'm going to untie you and let you get dressed. I washed your clothes, and they're laid out on the bed."

Glancing down, Alrec observed the black pants and shirt, thankful the woman was finally going to let him dress. Focusing back on her, he took note of her black clothing, which looked more tactical than the light linen she'd been wearing before. Maybe she'd fashioned them out of curtains too. The woman was resilient if nothing else.

"Once you're dressed, you're going to slip on these restraints." Holding up a cinched rope with two arm loops, she shook it. "Keep your hands behind your back. And then we're going to go walking. You need to increase your circulation if you're going to heal, and it's dark, so you won't burn to death."

"The restraints aren't necessary," he said, a slight plea in his voice. "I won't hurt you, Kilani."

She cocked an eyebrow. "Considering I met you on a battlefield when you were attacking my people, I'm a bit wary. Come on. The sooner you get dressed and bind yourself, the sooner we can walk. It's a clear night, and I'm craving fresh air. Let's go."

Standing, she tossed the rope so it landed on his clothes. Stuffing the knife in her belt, she untied his wrists and ankles before stepping back and crossing her arms over her pert breasts. Alrec allowed himself one glance at the supple skin that peeked above her neckline and then rose, accepting she was all business. Once he was dressed, he slipped each wrist through the binding behind his back.

"Thank you for cooperating," she said, striding over and tightening the ropes so they dug into his skin. "We're going to take it easy since your body has latched onto the poison. If you start to feel lightheaded, let me know."

He nodded, already craving the crisp night air upon his skin. She led them to the front door, closing it behind them and securing several locks. Then she began to walk toward the gurgling sounds from the nearby river, leaving him no choice but to follow.

They set a slow but steady pace, walking in step along the riverbank as the stars twinkled above. Alrec's muscles were stiff, but he would recover quickly. Such was the way of Vampyres, even with poison still lingering in his chest.

Glancing to the sky, Alrec noted the Star of Muthoni. Since it was the brightest in the sky, he could use it to calculate the distance back to Astaria.

"It's over four hundred miles to the east," Kilani said, gesturing with her head.

"What is?"

"Astaria. Do you think I'm dumb enough not to know you were calculating your way home?"

Grinning, he gazed at the crown of her golden hair, acknowledging the protective swell in his chest as she strode beside him. She was almost two heads shorter, the top of her head barely cresting his pecs. Etherya had created Vampyres to be much larger than Slayers, and he found himself wondering what it would be like to hold her small frame against his. Would she relax and snuggle into his muscular body, or would she remain stubborn and hold back? Would she trail kisses with those red lips over the path of scratchy hair that led to his most sensitive place or take him in her mouth? By the goddess, he could only imagine making love to her. Surely, she would be so tight she would squeeze every last cell of his shaft. He'd have to make sure his little one was slick and ready if that were to happen—

"Hey, where did you go?" she asked, snapping her fingers in his face.

Drawn from the lascivious musings, his lips curled. "Sorry. I was daydreaming. What did you say?"

"I asked how you're feeling. I have no problem sending you back to Astaria, but I want you to be one hundred percent first. One thing I hate is failing, and I'm not going to fail at your recovery."

"Failing isn't so bad," he mused. "Some would argue it's the best way to learn a lesson."

"Some?" she asked sardonically. "Are we to argue about this then?"

Chuckling, he longed to reach over and tuck away the strand of hair that grazed her cheek. Since his hands were bound, he settled for inhaling her scent, which seemed more intoxicating in the fresh air. "If you like. I think arguing with you would be quite fun."

"Oh, it's an experience all right. Just ask my father."

"Tell me about him," Alrec said, his tone open and curious. "I won't judge you, Kilani. You have my word."

Deep blue eyes studied him as the river gurgled beside them. "For some reason, I believe you," she finally said.

"Then tell me."

Sighing, she began the tale. One of unchangeable traditions and unyielding expectations. One where she had no say in her own life, or whom she would marry, or her destiny. It was a sad tale, and after she'd grown quiet, he understood why she'd chosen to live in solitude rather than live a life that would make her miserable.

"It's a choice few would make," Alrec said, his boots crunching leaves and branches as they walked. "Some would accuse you of being selfish for shunning a life of privilege and skirting your duty."

She stilled, inhaling a deep breath as she gazed at the dim horizon. "I guess some would."

"I, however, would not be one of those immortals." Halting, he turned to face her. "It's incredibly brave to live your truth even if others cannot see your vision. I find it quite admirable."

Turning, she lifted her gaze to his, something smoldering and simmering in the glowing orbs. Slowly lifting her hand, she gently touched his wound, safely dressed beneath a bandage and his black shirt. Her small fingers trailed over his pec, and a labored breath rushed from his lungs at the tender caress. His nipple grew hard and puckered under the fabric, and she lightly flicked it with her nail before gazing into his eyes.

"Careful, little one," he said, the deep baritone of his voice surrounding them. Tiny hairs stood to attention on her forearm, and he was pleased by her body's reaction to him. "I have let you restrain me because it makes you feel safe, but you know I could break free of these restraints if I wished."

Something flashed in her eyes as she skated her fingers up his chest, touching the tips to his pulsing vein and tracing it. "Is that a threat...or a promise?" she whispered.

A low growl exited his throat, causing her to gasp, and his shaft stood to attention at the shocked rush of air. "It's just a fact, little one."

Nodding, she lowered her hand to rest over his heart. The eight-chambered organ pulsed beneath her palm, and Alrec thanked the goddess he'd lived, if only so he could experience this one moment in the moonlight with his beautiful Slayer. Shallow breaths rushed through his lips as his body seemed to melt under her touch.

"I'd almost convinced myself your kind didn't have one," she murmured.

His eyebrows drew together. "Didn't have what?"

"A heart, Alrec," she said, the wistful words sending a jolt through his solar plexus. "I'd convinced myself your kind didn't have a heart."

Standing underneath the canopy of trees beside the gently rushing river, Alrec allowed her to absorb his heartbeats, longing for the day her lips would replace her hand atop the rapidly beating organ.

Chapter 10

Kilani continued to nurse Alrec, pleased he was healing more each day. As his body grew stronger, she knew it was futile to keep him restrained to the bed. He was a massive warrior, and even with his injuries, he could snap her in two without a thought. The fact he let her keep him restrained comforted her, and Kilani had so rarely been comforted. There wasn't much room for that when you were born into a family that put duty before love.

As Kilani continued to care for Alrec, she became quite surprised by his sense of humor. He would often tease her that she'd missed a spot after she changed his bandage or chide her for being so serious. Kilani would just roll her eyes and dismiss his playful jabs, although they brought her great pleasure deep within.

She'd never had an easy friendship with a man—hell, she'd rarely had an uneasy one—and she found it rather refreshing. Although it annoyed her that she enjoyed his company so much, she couldn't deny it made her...*happy*. The word had been foreign to her for so long, but the injured, chiding Vampyre had accomplished that task.

"Aren't you tired of sleeping on the couch?" he asked, dragging her from her thoughts as she smoothed the tape over his clean bandage. "I'm healed enough to sleep there. You'd have to untie me though." He arched a brow, and Kilani felt her cheeks warm at his heated gaze.

"My dear Vampyre," she said, resting her hand over his chest and blinking rapidly, "you should know by now you can't outsmart me. I thought you too sharp to try and outsmart a superior opponent."

Scoffing, he scrunched his features. "Perhaps I let you believe that so you'll keep putting your hands on me. It feels rather nice."

Kilani drew her hand away as if it were on fire and scowled at his resulting chuckle. "I'd rather stick my hand into a rattlesnake's belly."

Deep brown eyes assessed her, complete with the knowing smirk she found extremely sexy, and she struggled not to squirm under his gaze.

Finally, he opened those broad lips and asked, "Are the men of the Slayer kingdom completely daft? If I had the opportunity to court you and win your hand, I would try until my last breath."

A laugh bounded from her chest. "Wow, cheesy much?" Standing, she strode to the kitchen to rinse the cloth and drain some blood for his dinner. "And I'm a lot to take," she said, placing a glass on the island and slicing her inner forearm with a small knife before allowing the blood to fall. "I don't think Slayer men knew what to do with me. Slayer aristocrats anyway."

"Would you consider marrying a soldier or laborer?"

"Sure," she said, squeezing her arm to help the blood drain. "But my father would've had a conniption. That was a no-go as long as I lived in the kingdom."

"I've always found it so strange aristocrats look down on soldiers and laborers. We're the ones who protect them, allowing them to live their fancy lives."

"Hey, not all aristocrats feel that way." Holding a cloth to the cut, she allowed the blood to clot before wrapping it and securing the bandage. "I couldn't care less what station a man holds as long as he lets me fight. The Awakening...well, it *awakened* something in me, for lack of a better term." Clutching the glass, she padded over and sat on the edge of the bed. "I no longer wanted to wait for my life to

begin. I wanted to seize the day and fight."
Lifting the glass, she studied the blood in the
light of the nearby candle as her lips formed a
humorless smile. "Female soldiers hold no
value in my kingdom, so I can't see myself
finding a mate there. Until things change at
least." Extending the glass, she shuffled on the
bed and lifted it to his lips. "Dinnertime."

"Wait," he commanded softly, causing her to
still. "You are a magnificent woman, Kilani. It
was the first thought I had when I saw you
poised to kill me in a meadow all those years
ago."

Her eyebrows lifted. "You may be the only
one who thinks so."

"Then I'm glad you never found a mate. It
would be a shame for you to be tethered to a
man who didn't understand your worth."

Left unspoken between them was the
obvious sentiment that *he* understood her
worth...and the almost tangible energy that
always seemed to sizzle between them when
they slipped into these more serious
discussions. Uncomfortable, she touched the
glass to his lips. "Come on. I can't have you
waste away before I kick you out. Drink."

His lips surrounded the rim of the glass,
and her throat grew dry as they moved on the
crystal as he drank. The motions were erotic,
spurring images of him fastening those full
lips to her breast and closing them around her

nipple. Would he gaze into her eyes—as he was now—while he worked his lips over her sensitive flesh?

Overcome by the vision, she tilted the glass, forcing him to finish so she could return to the kitchen. The heat of his body seemed to envelop her, and she suddenly felt the urge to run.

"Thank you," he murmured when she lowered the glass. "Your blood is the finest I've ever had, but I wish you didn't have to harm yourself to feed me."

"Oh, it's fine," she said, breathless as she stood and ran a hand through her hair. "I'm tough and have handled worse, believe me."

She began to wash the glass, cognizant of his gaze as he stayed mute in the bed. Frazzled, she set the glass on the cloth to dry and glanced around the kitchen, desperate for another activity so she could shift the focus.

"There is a way you could feed me and it won't hurt."

Facing him, she placed her hands on her hips, knowing she shouldn't take the bait. "Like I said, it's fine."

"You could let me drink from you, Kilani," he said, his voice mesmerizing as his gaze drilled into hers. "I would lick your wrist, coating it in my self-healing saliva, which would prevent the pain. Then I would pierce you with my fangs, drink, and lick the wounds closed. It's how we were designed after all. The decree that Vampyres cannot drink directly from Slayers came from immortals, not from Etherya."

"The immortal rulers made that decree because direct drinking allows a Vampyre to read and absorb a Slayer's thoughts and mental images," she said, her tone flat. "And if you think I'm going to let you read my mind, you've definitely lost yours."

His soft laugh filtered through the room. "I won't say getting you to divulge the secret you know about the Deamon weakness hasn't crossed my mind, but I assure you, there's nothing nefarious about my proposal."

"Nothing nefarious," she repeated, her tone droll.

"I'm the one who's restrained here, little one." He tugged at the ropes. "You have the upper hand."

"And I'd like to keep it that way, thank you very much." Finished with the discussion that had somehow turned her knees to jelly, she walked to the closet by the front door and threw on her shawl. "I'm heading to the garden. Need to gather some of my own food so I can keep feeding you. It's a vicious cycle, keeping you alive. I might decide to let you die tomorrow."

"Kilani," he drawled in a teasing, sultry tone that sent shivers of arousal down her spine.

"Did I ruffle your feathers, little one? Perhaps you're as excited at the thought of me drinking from your wrist as I am." He waggled his brows. "Or I could drink from your neck. I think that might be even more exciting, no?"

Gritting her teeth, she shot him a glare, annoyed he was calling attention to her unwanted attraction. Vampyres had heightened senses for arousal, and she had no doubt he could smell the slickness that was rapidly coating her inner thighs under his unwavering gaze. Frustrated, she pivoted and stalked outside, slamming the door behind her.

Unfortunately, the sound of his desire-laden chuckle followed her to the garden and lingered as she toiled under the bright sun.

Chapter 11

Kilani fell into a pattern with Alrec as the wounds on his chest healed quicker each day. After a week, the red welts had all but disappeared, and she found herself melancholy at the fact he would soon leave and return to Astaria.

"You know, I'm starting to dig the bondage thing you have going on here," Alrec said, his tone sardonic as she sat beside him, dragging a wet cloth over his chest. "But we both know I'm healed, Kilani." Tugging on the ropes, he flashed a grin, his fangs gently pushing into his lower lip.

Her ministrations ceased as she studied the black hairs on his chest, darker than the thick brown hair atop his head. "I guess you're right. And you've been nothing but gracious on our nightly walks. I would even venture to say we're becoming...*friends*." She mimicked gagging, causing Alrec to chuckle. "It's a tough pill to swallow, being friends with a Vampyre. The world has gone mad." Rising, she trailed to the kitchen to wash the cloth before spreading it over the rim of the sink to dry.

"I am honored to be your friend," he murmured, causing her heart to slam at his genuine tone.

Placing her hands on the sink, Kilani stared out the small window, acknowledging how much she cherished this time of day. Dusk had become the linchpin of her existence, when she would untie Alrec, bind his hands behind his back, and they would take their nightly walks by the river.

In the days that had passed, they had discussed their histories and told each other their stories. She'd learned that he'd never been in love, although several Vampyre women had certainly tried to catch his affection. He spoke of them fondly but took his vow to protect his people seriously, and that had always taken precedence.

Although he was now alone upon Etherya's Earth, as was she, he wasn't lonely. Instead, he revered his family for dying noble deaths in the Awakening and strove to be a great warrior. It was admirable, and Kilani was perplexed at how easily he'd wormed his way into her stubborn heart and earned her respect.

"What's that smile for?" he asked softly from the bed.

Sighing, she padded over and studied him, rubbing her arms as she debated. "It's time for our walk. I'm contemplating not binding your hands tonight. Is that a mistake?"

Laughing, he shook his head. "I'll be a perfect gentleman. You have my word."

Gnawing her lip, she acknowledged unbinding him would put them on even ground. No longer would she have the upper hand, nor could they pretend she was in control. Whether they voiced the obvious or not, it was evident Alrec could overpower her and instantly kill her if he wished.

"I'm trusting you," she whispered, reaching to untie his wrists.

Solemn brown eyes stared deep into hers. "Thank you, little one."

Kilani swallowed, annoyed as the image of him whispering the endearment in her ear as he loomed above her in the large bed flashed through her mind. Making quick work of his binds, she busied herself in the kitchen while he dressed, only sneaking the occasional glance at his magnificent ass. After all, she was a red-blooded Slayer and hadn't been so attracted to a man in centuries. The fact he was a Vampyre should've alarmed her, but since it didn't, she just allowed herself to enjoy the view.

They headed outside and began to trek along the river. Alrec asked her basic questions, and she did so in return, and the conversation flowed as it always did between them. As they strolled, curiosity welled until she could no longer contain it.

"It's hard for me to believe you've never been in love. Don't you want to bond and have a family one day?"

His eyebrows lifted as he grinned. "Have we finally gotten to the point where we discuss our dreams and fears? That seems quite personal for two mortal enemies, no?"

"Forget it," she said, rolling her eyes. "I was just wondering—"

"I'm teasing you, Kilani." His warm fingers ran over her forearm before he slid his palm over hers and laced their fingers. "You are quite serious for a Slayer. I thought you were supposed to be the carefree species."

"We were until the world fell apart," she muttered, unable to stop herself from squeezing his fingers, noting how perfect they felt laced with hers. "It changed my perspective, and now I can't even remember what carefree means."

His gentle laughter washed over her, spurring a reflexive grin.

"Why are you laughing?"

"I was just thinking that perhaps I should remind you what it means to be carefree," he said, the silken tone of his voice causing tiny bumps to rise on her forearms. "I can think of several activities we could try."

"I'm sure you can," she said, arching a sardonic brow. "But let's get back to the question. Are you trying to avoid my grilling?"

His footsteps halted, and he gently tugged her hand, turning her to face him. Stepping closer, he lifted his free hand and tenderly grazed her jaw. Cupping it, he ran his thumb over her cheek, the caress mesmerizing as he spoke softly in the moonlight.

"I always felt I would fall in love with someone both fierce and tender. As a warrior, I need a partner who can understand my calling to protect my people and balance that with affection. Vampyres don't allow females in the army, so I've never met a woman who possesses both..." His words trailed off as his thumb inched toward her lips, gently brushing them as she stood frozen... mesmerized...enchanted...

"Don't say it," she whispered.

His full lips curved. "Don't say 'until you'?" Shaking his head, he leaned closer. "I would never. It's incredibly lame, and I can't chance dousing your attraction to me. Your glances at my ass as I dress are the only thing keeping me going."

Kilani's mouth fell open, and she swatted his chest. "I do not glance at your ass!"

Chuckling, he tilted his head. "Warriors are supposed to be better liars, Kilani. We'll have to work on that."

His hand slid to her jaw again, and she bit her lip, knowing she was busted. Placing her hand over his heart, she noted the strong beats pulsing in tandem with her own as arousal swirled between them.

"We can't," she whispered.

"Why not?" was his silken response, his handsome features laced with mischief and desire.

"Because we're different species—"

"The logistics are the same. Trust me."

"And how do you know? How many Slayers have you slept with?"

Breathing a laugh, he shook his head. "None, but I'm willing to break the streak."

Expelling a breath, she tightened her fingers on his chest as acceptance coursed through her pulsing frame. Hell, she hadn't truly experienced joy in so long. Giving herself to this Vampyre, to this man who'd spared her life years ago, was reckless and impulsive...and perhaps it was *exactly* what she needed. After all, what was the point in living a life you chose if you never felt any bliss? If you never allowed yourself one moment of pleasure or gratification?

"I see your wheels turning, little one," he chimed, gently tapping her forehead. "I don't make this decision lightly either. Never in a million years would I have imagined I'd become consumed with a Slayer. But here we are, and it seems foolish to squander the opportunity."

"Consumed with me, huh?" she teased, her eyes darting between his. "Perhaps you're only placating me because I saved your life."

Releasing her hand, he slid his palm across her lower back, pulling her close until there was nothing between them but desire. Splaying his fingers, he gently cupped her ass, molding his body to hers before lowering his head and grazing her nose with his.

"I was consumed with you the moment I saw you planted in a field with fire in your eyes and a weapon clutched in your hand, ready to defend your people. I never forgot you, Kilani."

"This is insane," she breathed against his lips. "We're supposed to hate each other—"

"For one night, let's forget what we're *supposed* to do and just feel. Can you do that for me, little one?"

Something sticky and stifling coursed through her veins, and she struggled to dissect it until she realized it was...*fear.* All she'd known for years was her solitary life in the woods. If she gave herself to this man, would she suddenly begin to crave more? Living without affection and companionship when you couldn't experience them was one thing. Living without them after you'd immersed yourself in them was daunting... perhaps even dangerous.

"I can't allow myself the luxury of craving something I can never have."

Resting his forehead against hers, he stared deep into her eyes. "Then you'll have to find a way to have everything you desire."

Even as her brain told her she was making a mistake, she slid her arms around his neck and lifted to her toes. "I don't think that's possible," she murmured.

"Do you want me to kiss you, little one? To carry you home and make love to you?" He brushed a tender kiss across her lips. "All you have to do is ask."

Tightening her arms around his neck, she pressed her body against his, reveling in his desire-laden growl. Still unsure, she dug her fingers into his neck, arousal gushing between her thighs at his resulting groan.

"I want you to kiss me," she whispered, closing her eyes as she held on for dear life. "Let's start there—"

The words were consumed by his strong lips and wet tongue as it swept them away with one smooth stroke. Throwing caution to the wind, Kilani relaxed in her Vampyre's

arms and allowed herself to enjoy the
moment.

Chapter 12

Alrec clutched his little Slayer, disbelief entwining with arousal as it snaked through his veins. Never did he imagine he'd be granted the opportunity to kiss her...to taste her...but now that he'd touched her, he wondered if he could ever truly let go.

Small, wanton purrs exited her throat, igniting his arousal as he reminded himself to go slow. If it were up to him, he'd lower her lithe body to the soft grass and lick every drop of arousal from between her thighs before slicking her up again and burying himself deep inside. Knowing she wasn't ready, he focused on kissing her, thanking the goddess a million times for his good fortune.

Her tongue slid over his, coating him with her taste, and his body shook with arousal at the ardent strokes. Longing to please her, he swiped his tongue over hers before sucking it between his lips. A deep moan rumbled through his belly as he sucked her, overcome with her sultry whimpers and the sharp points of her nails digging into his neck.

Releasing her tongue, he trailed soft kisses over her wet lips and firm jaw before resting his mouth on the shell of her ear. "You taste so good, little one," he breathed, pleased when she shivered in his arms. "I want to lick you everywhere."

"Alrec," she murmured, sliding her fingers in his thick hair and gently tugging, urging him to meet her gaze. "I can't become attached to you." Solemn blue eyes swirled with fear, affection, and longing as she stared back at him.

"Are you so sure that would end in doom, little one?" Delving his fingers into her soft hair, he stroked the silken tresses as their labored breaths mingled. "Even if you're convinced you're smarter than me, you're not a fortune-teller, are you?"

Laughter gurgled from her throat. "Seeing the future is one skill I don't have."

"Then let's take this day by day and live in the moment. Our lives are long, Kilani. It won't hurt to take a small sliver of time to focus on what's between us."

Blue orbs darted between his. "But you need to go back to Astaria. You have a duty."

"I do," he said with a nod, "and I will fulfill it for eternity when I return. But eternity is long, and I want to make sure I carry the memory of you with me."

"Damn," she whispered, shaking her head. "That's so freaking romantic. Who knew Vampyres were so sappy?" She flashed a cheeky grin.

"I'm only sappy for women who save my life and threaten to kill me, all in the same day," he teased, palming her cheek and winking as she chuckled.

White teeth toyed with her lip as she pondered. "How long do you want to stay?"

Alrec's features drew together. "I want to be strong for my trek back to Astaria. It's possible I'll encounter Deamons on the way, and I want to be prepared to fight them. Perhaps I could stay a few weeks and we could train together at night. You could ensure I'm in top form before I leave."

"So, you're only interested in my battle skills?" She wrinkled her nose, adorable as she teased him.

"I'm interested in so much more, but we'll start with the sparring." He chucked her nose, thoroughly enjoying their banter. "But to be clear, I want to make love to you, Kilani. I'm going to employ all my swagger to entice you into bed." He waggled his eyebrows.

The smooth skin of her throat gleamed in the moonlight as she tossed her head back and laughed. Overwhelmed by her beauty, he lowered his lips to the pulsing vein and peppered it with tender kisses. She sighed, clutching his shoulders as he loved her.

"And if you'll let me, I'll drink from you here while I'm inside you, Kilani." The words crackled with lust and affection as he drew the soft skin between his lips and gently sucked. Her knees buckled, and he held her tight, pulling her skin back and forth between his lips as she writhed against him.

"Oh, god..."

"Yes, sweetheart," he murmured, licking the spot, now red and tender from his ministrations. "All you have to do is ask."

A low, sexy groan rumbled in her chest, and she lifted her lids to latch onto his gaze. "I'll think about it. In the meantime, I like the idea of sparring with you. I want you to be ready to defend yourself...and I might like the idea of kicking your ass every night."

Alrec scoffed and nipped her nose. "I never knew delusion was sexy until now."

She swatted him as he chuckled.

"But yes, it's smart to retrain my body before I leave. And I can't wait to have you flat on your back with a spear to your throat so I can force you to tell me the Deamon intel."

"Never gonna happen," she said, drawing back and gripping his hand. "You live in la-la land, my friend, but I'll allow it." Threading their fingers, she tugged, urging him to resume the walk. Alrec fell into step beside her and immersed himself in the moment. One day, many centuries from now, he would remember the night he first kissed his beautiful Slayer by the gently rushing river under a ribbon of stars.

Unable to squelch his grin, he strolled with Kilani until they grew tired and returned to the cabin. Alrec undressed down to his underwear and lay on the couch, silently offering Kilani the bed. Hours later, he gazed over, comforted by her gentle snores and the sight of her wrapped in the sheets... determined to earn his place by her side in the bed before he had to make the long journey home.

Chapter 13

Kilani threw herself into training with Alrec, thrilled to have a worthy sparring partner after so many years alone. She'd done her best to keep her skills sharp since there were always looming threats in a world as consumed with war as Etherya's Earth. Although she was far from civilization, a stray band of Deamons could always stumble upon her cabin, and she needed to be prepared.

She also wanted Alrec strong for his trip home since it would be a several-week journey and he could encounter many different threats. Although she'd vowed to stay unattached to her handsome Vampyre, deep down Kilani knew she was fooling herself. His kisses along the riverbank had set her body on fire, and his tender words murmured against her skin had almost melted her heart.

Each day, they drew closer to the point where she would shed her reservations and let him make love to her. Kilani already knew this was a foregone conclusion, but she appreciated the respectful way he kept his distance, showcasing his honor. His respect for her was almost as attractive as those sexy fangs and luscious ass. *Almost.*

A few nights after their first kiss, Kilani stood firm on the soft grass, a spear clutched in each hand as she gritted her teeth. Alrec faced her, breath rushing from his lungs as he held his own spear. Kilani had fashioned them for fishing, but they were also perfect for sparring with a hulking Vampyre. Opening her lips, Kilani emitted a grunt before rushing toward her opponent, their spears held high in the air.

Alrec anticipated her move, blocking her weapons with his own before rotating and swiping at her shins. Reading his movements, Kilani jumped, avoiding the weapon and backing away. Alrec advanced and lunged, and they began a series of deft blows, the wooden spears clanking in the warm night air as the skirmish raged on. Eventually, Alrec's height advantage became too much for her skill, and he caught her wrist, holding it high.

"Yield," he commanded, his warm breaths rushing over her face. "I have the advantage."

"No fucking way!" she gritted, thrusting the spear in her free hand high. Uttering a curse, he dropped his spear and grabbed her other wrist. Holding her still, he gazed into her eyes.

"Yield, little one."

"The Deamons you encounter on your way back to Astaria aren't going to yield," she said, trying to twirl away from his grasp. "So I'm not either—"

Alrec lurched, quick as lightning, surrounding her waist with one arm before slamming her to the ground. Although she knew he took care not to hurtle her too hard, the breath was knocked from her lungs as he loomed above her.

"Yield, woman," he said, yanking both spears from her hands as he shifted over her, pinning her to the ground with his large body. Gripping one of the spears, he held the tip to her throat. Kilani glared into his eyes, equal parts furious he'd gotten the upper hand and aroused as hell at the gorgeous man who now held a deadly weapon to her throat.

"Damn, this is so hot," she whispered, breathless as she lay below him.

Breathing a laugh, he nodded. "So fucking hot." Pressing the spear to her neck, he leaned closer, barely brushing her nose with his. "Tell me the Deamon weakness, little one."

Kilani made a *tsk tsk* sound and shook her head, her hair grazing over the grass. "Not until you earn it." Grunting, she reached for the spear that lay just within her reach and sliced it through the air until the tip rested at his neck. "Looks like we're at an impasse."

Alrec's lips curved before he tossed his weapon aside and slid his arm under her body. Rolling them over, he relaxed on his back as she sat atop him. "Go ahead and stab me," he said, eyes twinkling as he placed his hands beneath his head. "I'm enjoying the view."

A muted chuckle escaped before she threw her spear aside and planted her palms on his chest. "You like the woman on top, huh?"

"Sweetheart, I'll take you in any way and from any direction I can have you," was his silken reply.

Kilani licked the suddenly dry roof of her mouth, wondering if she'd ever met a sexier man. She'd had a few lovers in her past— mostly aristocratic men who were boring as hell and handsome in their regal, austere ways —but her Vampyre was masculine and...*raw*, with those sexy fangs, deep brown eyes, and the thick hair she longed to clench between her fingers as she took him deep inside her body. And that ass... Good lord, she loved his ass.

Glancing toward the sky, she noticed the first trickle of dawn easing over the horizon. Patting his chest, she stood and offered her hand. "Come on. You might have bested me, but I don't think you'll best the sun."

Alrec took her hand, and she pulled him to his feet before they gathered the weapons and trailed home. Once there, they removed their shirts and pants, and Kilani washed away the grime, aware of his heated glances as he did the same beside her in the small kitchen.

Alrec stood silent beside her, a question in his gaze as he waited for her to move. Kilani's eyes darted over his firm chest and thick thighs sprinkled with coarse hair before landing on his erection, which was now pushing against the fabric of his underwear. Swallowing thickly, she debated the consequences of her actions, understanding she would most likely develop feelings for him if they made love. He was everything she would've chosen in a man if she'd had the ability to choose one when living at Uteria.

A warrior who embraced her desire to fight instead of shunning it.

A handsome man with gentle eyes and a kind heart.

A man who made her laugh and feel safe, and desired her even though they were worlds apart.

And...he was a fucking Vampyre. In all her musings, Kilani had never imagined her ideal mate would be a damn Vampyre.

"What are you thinking, little one?" he asked softly, still frozen as he waited for her to choose for both of them.

Stepping forward, she was enveloped by the heat emanating from his strong frame as she slid a hand over his ass, gently cupping him through the fabric. "I'm thinking that you're really lucky you have this ass. Because it's hindering my ability to think logically, and I'm about to make a really important decision."

Desire sparked in his eyes as he drew closer. "What decision, Kilani?"

Spearing her nails into the taut muscles of his ass, she gave a sultry laugh at his resulting hiss. "My dear Vampyre," she drawled, stepping closer and rising to her toes, "I'm going to ask you to make love to me—"

And then, all words ceased to exist as her eager lover cemented his lips to hers and lifted her in his arms before carrying her to bed.

Chapter 14

Alrec carried his little Slayer to bed, gently placing her on the turned-down sheets as she gazed at him with lust and affection. Her blond hair fanned over the pillow, and he took a moment to bask in her beauty.

"Kilani," he whispered, stretching over her and running a finger over the soft skin of her cheek. "You're so beautiful, sweetheart."

Sliding her hands around his neck, she drew him close and brushed a sweet kiss over his lips. "Show me." Her nails impaled his shoulders, causing him to groan. "I haven't done this in a long time. I hope I remember how." Biting her lip, she grinned, adorable in the dim light of the candles she'd lit when they returned home.

"I'll remind you," he murmured, pecking her lips before trailing tender kisses over her neck. Her melodious laughter surrounded them, and Alrec knew he would hear the sound in his dreams long after he returned home. Pressing kisses to her flushed skin, he made his way to the valley between her breasts. Gliding his hands under her back, he unhooked her bra and slid it from her body, dropping it to the floor as he gazed at her pert nipples.

"Careful with the bra," she rasped, closing her eyes as he cupped one of her breasts in his palm. "It's the only one I have."

"Then perhaps I will destroy it so I can see these pretty breasts more often." Grazing his thumb over her nipple, he reveled in her gasp as the tiny bud grew taut. Lowering his head, he murmured, "Open your eyes, little one."

Those midnight blue orbs drifted open, and Alrec felt a jolt of awareness in his solar plexus. By the goddess, he'd never been so consumed with a woman. His only wish was to please her—to imprint their lovemaking in her mind so she would remember him long after he returned to a life without her. Sadness swamped him at the thought, so he pushed it away to focus on his little Slayer.

Opening his mouth, he rimmed her nipple with his lips, mesmerized by the emotion in her gaze and her reddened cheeks. Closing his lips around the taut bud, he began to suck her, the motions smooth and methodic as her nipple peaked against his tongue.

"Oh...*god*..." she moaned, threading her fingers through his hair, clutching tight as he loved her. Alrec smiled around her supple flesh, pleased at her soft purrs of pleasure. Sucking her deep one last time, he gently kissed the taut nub before drifting to her other breast and repeating the same torturous, tender ministrations.

"Feels so good..." she murmured, head tossing on the pillow. "Holy shit, I'm so freaking turned on. From a Vampyre...never would've thought...*aarrgh*..."

Chuckling, Alrec sucked her nipple several more times before drawing back and flicking it with his tongue. The deft motions sent a flush across her pale skin, and her back bowed upon the bed. The scent of her arousal permeated the room, and Alrec's body began to quiver with the intense need to taste her.

Rising to his knees, he stared deep into her eyes as he hooked his fingers in the waistband of her panties. Silently asking permission, a swell of desire rocked his frame when she bit her finger and nodded against the pillow. Gaze cemented to hers, he slid the garment from her body. Placing his palms on her inner thighs, he spread her wide, emitting a low groan at the slick that covered her deepest place.

"Sweetheart," he whispered, gently running the pads of his thumbs over her wet upper thighs. "Look at you."

The little imp grinned and pushed into his thumbs, causing Alrec to grit his teeth. Dying to taste her, he lowered between her legs, pushing them wide with his shoulders so he could burrow into her deepest place. Spreading her wet folds wide, he touched his tongue to her drenched opening. Gazing deep into her stunning eyes, he swiped a broad stroke over her pussy, from her core to the tight little nub at the top of her mound, and relished her deep moan as she squirmed against him.

"Alrec..."

"Yes, little one," he rasped against her trembling skin. "Push against me. I've never tasted anything as sweet. I'm going to lick away every drop."

Her resulting moan enveloped him, urging him on as he lost himself in the most pleasurable moment of his life. Nothing in all his centuries upon Etherya's Earth compared to having his strong, gorgeous Slayer open before him as he feasted. Determined to make her scream, he began a series of deep, sweeping strokes along her folds, imbibing her honeyed-essence.

As her whimpers grew more fervent, he latched onto her gaze and spread her wide, impaling his tongue in her tight opening as he placed two fingers on the swollen nub at the top of her slit. Entranced by her, he surged his tongue inside, back and forth, as he circled his fingers on her clit, applying firm, meticulous pressure.

Kilani writhed upon the bed, tightening her legs around his shoulders, and he knew she was close. Consumed by desire for her, he moaned against her core as her body began a series of deep trembles. Closing her eyes, his little Slayer tossed back her head and began to come. Hoping to send her to heaven, Alrec continued his motions, overcome with lust and emotion.

Violent tremors shook her lithe frame until she began to laugh and constricted her legs around his head. The action forced him deeper against her center, and he began to laugh as well, ceasing the motions of his tongue and fingers so she could experience the high before falling back to earth.

"Holy good grief!" she cried, clutching the covers at each side as her body quaked and shuddered. "Help..."

Chuckling, Alrec placed a kiss on her mound before rising to cover her with his now trembling body. His shaft was painfully erect inside his underwear, and he wanted nothing more than to plunge it inside her satiated body. Palming her cheek, he studied her flushed face, grinning when she opened her eyes and swatted him.

"Why did you do that?" she asked, the words breathless and weak. "I was used to my own hand, and now you've ruined that."

"I want to ruin you, little one," he murmured, pressing his lips to hers and plunging his tongue deep into her wet mouth. Their tongues slid over each other's, Alrec's still coated with her sweet honey, and she uttered a low, satisfied groan. "I want you to remember me after I'm gone."

Gazing at him with eyes full of emotion, she threaded her fingers through his hair. "I think that's a given."

"Good." Placing a peck on her nose, Alrec shifted and drew off his underwear. Aligning himself back over her body, he placed his leg between hers, opening her wide and lowering his fingers to her core.

"Let's get you slick and ready again so I can fuck you."

A ragged breath escaped her lips as she pushed against his fingers, undulating into them as he circled her swollen clit. Unable to look away from her gorgeous eyes, Alrec slipped a finger inside her tight channel, loving her resulting mewl. After dragging it back and forth in the taut vise, he added another, gauging her reaction.

"It's going to be tight," she said, teeth digging into her lower lip as she grinned.

"Oh, I'm counting on it." Sliding over her, he removed his fingers and glided the tip of his shaft to her opening. Inhaling deeply, he glided the sensitive head through her wet folds, closing his eyes at the extreme pleasure. Clenching his jaw, he reminded himself to go slow so he didn't hurt her—a massive feat since his body was ready to mount her and fuck her straight through the headboard.

"What are you smiling at?"

Lifting his lids, he slid his fingers through her hair and softly clenched. "At how hard I want to fuck you. But I'll be gentle. Ready, little one?"

Her chest rose with a deep inhale as she nodded. "Ready."

Lowering his forehead to hers, he gazed into those limitless eyes as he began to push inside. Kilani clenched his shoulders, drawing him deep as the pricks of pain from her fingernails drove him wild. Determined not to hurt her, he went slow, dying a small death each time her wet walls surrounded another inch of his sensitive flesh.

"Open up to me, sweetheart," he whispered against her lips. "You can let go. It will feel better, trust me."

Her swollen lips fell open as her muscles melted beneath him, and Alrec took advantage, surging inside her tight channel. Overwhelmed with bliss, he began to drag his cock back and forth through her core, striving to reach the spot deep within that would make her scream.

"Tell me what you need, Kilani."

"Deeper..." she moaned. "Harder...oh, just don't stop..."

Encouraged by the desirous words, Alrec slid his hand from her hair to her shoulder, cupping to hold her in place. Groaning her name, he began to stroke her deepest place with his cock, his hips undulating at a furious pace as sweat beaded on his brow.

"Yesssss..." she hissed, her body open and trembling beneath him. "You're so far inside me...I feel everything..."

Vowing to hit the spot that would send her into euphoria, Alrec pounded her tight channel, coating his sensitive flesh in her honeyed slick as the plushy folds threatened to wring him dry. Closing his eyes, he felt the tingling at his lower back and the tightening of his balls. Knowing he would only last a few more seconds, he rested his lips on her neck, sucking her fragrant skin deep before murmuring into her nape.

"Come again, little one... Come around my cock..."

Drawing her flesh between lips, he sucked her as she writhed beneath him. The head of his cock jutted against a spot deep within her luscious body, finally sending her over the edge. Piercing his shoulders with her nails, she cried his name before her spine snapped, her body devolving into a furious round of quakes against him. Burying his face in her neck, Alrec tightened his hold before letting go, feeling his release shoot down his cock and begin to spurt into her gorgeous body. Lost in the moment, he flooded her with his essence, marking her as his as pulses of desire leaped from his body to mingle with hers. Groaning with pleasure, he shuddered against her, emptying every last piece of himself into his little Slayer. Unable to focus on breathing or moving or...anything that required energy, he snuggled into her, hoping like hell he wasn't crushing her.

Kilani wriggled against him, their bodies entwined as the sweat from their exertion cooled their sated frames. Sighing, she ran her hand over the welts on his shoulders.

"I think I drew blood," she muttered softly, rubbing the marks that would soon self-heal. "Sorry."

Breathing a laugh, Alrec ran the tip of his nose along her neck, inhaling her fragrant scent. "Don't mind. You can pierce me anytime, Kilani."

Gliding her arms around his shoulders, she clutched him close, sliding a silken thigh over his. Alrec was wrapped in her like the most precious present, and he never wanted to let go. Kissing her temple, he asked, "Do you need me to move?"

She shook her head, snuggling deeper into their embrace. "Feels good. I just want to lie here with you inside me for a while. Is that okay?"

"Mm-hmm." After placing reverent kisses on her silken hair, he rested his cheek on the pillow. Since they were different species, there was no chance of pregnancy or transmitting disease, so he was content to lie with her and commit the moment to memory. Relaxing against her, he softly stroked her hair upon the pillow as their breathing grew heavy.

"It's a vestigial third eye," she murmured against his chest.

"Hmm?"

"The Deamon weakness. They have a vestigial third eye between their eyebrows that never evolved. It's a vulnerable spot that allows them to be killed instantly if struck."

Alrec swallowed the emotion in his throat, understanding the admission was more than just intel on an enemy species. It was proof she trusted him, that she saw him as her equal...perhaps even as her partner in a world where they both were quite alone.

"Thank you," he whispered, kissing her forehead. "I'd like to hear more tomorrow, especially on how you found this out. Do you hang out with Deamons I'm not aware of?"

Chuckling, she licked his sweaty chest, causing him to shiver. "No, but I'm pretty observant and have run into a few Deamons since I left Uteria. I'll tell you everything tomorrow."

Unable to hold his eyes open, he allowed them to drift shut as her evergreen scent filled his nostrils. "Can't wait. I was honored to love you like this, Kilani. Sweet dreams, little one."

Her leg tightened around him as she drew him closer. "I was honored to be loved by you. Good night, Alrec."

Losing himself in the warmth of her sated body, Alrec succumbed to sleep.

Chapter 15

Kilani slid out of bed several hours later, leaving her sleeping Vampyre twisted in the sheets as he snored. After cleaning the remnants of their tryst from her thighs, she dressed and headed outside. The afternoon sun was bright, and she smirked at how well she'd acclimated to Alrec's schedule. Since he could only go outside at night, Kilani had been sleeping during the day and using nights to train with him. As long as he lived in her home, she would adhere to that schedule. There was plenty of time to reverse it when he was gone.

Frowning at the thought, she entered the wooden outhouse that had always existed behind the house. Curiosity still lingered about who'd built the cabin, but so far, Kilani hadn't found any clues. Perhaps it would always remain a mystery. Since her life was rather uneventful—barring the most recent events—she welcomed the small dash of intrigue.

Wincing as she stepped inside and closed the door, she acknowledged the soreness between her legs. After all, Alrec was massive, and he'd certainly stretched her with that magnificent cock. Sighing as she took care of business, she let the memories wash over her.

After picking some vegetables in the garden, she headed inside to find Alrec in the kitchen, clad in his underwear as he ran a wet cloth over his upper body.

"I see you're making use of the poor man's shower situation I have going on here," she teased, setting the vegetables on the counter.

"The basins of water are serviceable, but have you ever thought of searching for a well to tap and installing plumbing?" he asked, dipping the cloth in the basin and wringing it before wiping the back of his neck.

Shrugging, she began to wash the vegetables. "Someday. After all, I have an eternity to figure out how to rig the plumbing."

Brooding eyes assessed her as he finished dragging the cloth over his skin. After laying it flat to dry, he strode over and lifted her hand. "Good evening," he said softly, kissing her knuckles.

"I'm used to 'good morning,' but I guess your kind does prefer 'good evening.'"

"We would prefer to walk in the sun again, but I don't foresee that happening for quite a while. As you noted, there is so much hatred to overcome."

Tilting her head, her lips curved into a sad smile. "Perhaps one day things will change and we can help chart a new path. One where Slayers and Vampyres live in peace again."

"I hope so. Although the species have remained separate, there could even come a day when they choose to intermarry."

Laughter bounded from her throat. "Who knew you were such a dreamer? I can't ever see that happening."

"Stranger things have happened in our world, Kilani," he murmured, winking before releasing her hand and trailing over to the couch to dress. "One day, you might eat your words."

"If the immortal world ever reaches that level of peace, I will happily admit you were right. For now, I'll continue to live in reality. Let me wash these and eat some dinner before the sun goes down, and then we can spar."

Grinning at his optimism, Kilani got to work preparing the food. Two hours later, they strolled to the riverbank to spar under the full moon.

"How did you learn about the vestigial third eye?" Alrec asked when they took a break.

"Thankfully, my cabin has remained off the radar from Deamons, but when I first moved here, I ventured quite far to survey the land. I came across a cluster of Deamons and listened to their conversation."

Dragging the spear over the ground absently, she mimicked the Deamon's voice, low and gravelly. *"Make sure the Vampyre bastards don't pierce you between the eyes. You'll die instantly."* Shrugging, she tilted her head. "It was good intel. Perhaps there's a weapon the Vampyres or Slayers can create to take advantage."

"No doubt," Alrec said with a nod. "I'll make sure to pass along the intel to Commander Latimus when I return home. Thank you, Kilani."

Lifting her spear, she arched a brow. "Don't think because I gave you the goods I'm going to go easy on you. Come on, Vampyre. I still want to kick that fine ass a few times tonight."

Chuckling, Alrec clutched his weapon and set his feet. "Come on then," he taunted, hooking his fingers. "Show me what you've got, little one."

Blissful laughter echoed along with their grunts under the dark clouds, and Kilani fought with all her might, although her worthy opponent would always best her in the end. After several hours of training, her hulking Vampyre gently urged her to the soft grass, tugging at their clothes until there was nothing between them but the warm night air.

Giving in to her passion, Kilani made love for the first time under a swath of twinkling stars.

Chapter 16

T he next night, after a grueling sparring
session, Kilani and Alrec headed inside
two hours before dawn to rest. Exhausted, she
didn't have the energy to make love. Unsure
how to tell Alrec, she lay down in bed, feeling
her eyes begin to drift closed.

"I'm so tired tonight," she said, yawning as
she snuggled into the pillow. "I'm sorry..."

"It's okay, sweetheart." Leaning over, he
kissed her temple and smoothed her hair.
"Get some rest. I'll be here when you wake up."

She thought he might crawl into bed and
hold her, but the thought drifted away as she
fell into slumber. Over an hour later, she
awoke, snaking an arm over the mattress to
search for Alrec but finding it empty. Sitting
up, she pushed her hair out of her face as he
strode in through the door carrying an armful
of what looked to be...sticks? Bamboo?

"What are you doing?" she asked, wondering if she was still dreaming.

"Hello, sleeping beauty. Did you rest well?" Setting the wood in the corner, he stalked over and kissed her forehead.

"Uh...yeah, but...what are you doing?"

"I'm going to use the bamboo to make some piping for you," he said, gesturing with his head toward the pile. "And then I'm going to tap a well and create a well pump for you before I leave. At least this will leave you with a basic form of indoor plumbing."

Kilani's heart all but melted at his genuine expression and lopsided smile. "You're going to install plumbing for me?"

"Yes," he said, chuckling as he nodded. "I know it might not be as romantic as flowers or jewelry—"

"It's perfect," she interjected, rising to her knees and throwing her arms around his neck. Plopping an ardent kiss on his face, she sighed. "My hero. I'll take plumbing over jewelry any day. Thank you."

"You're welcome." Pecking her lips, he grinned. "Had I known plumbing would've garnered this reaction, I would've installed it several days ago."

"Oh, stop," she said, swatting his chest. "This is amazing. I'll help you."

"I'll need to sand the inside of the bamboo stalks to make sure they're uniform and don't leak. I think I can find some makeshift things around the house to use to construct a pump. It's not going to be the most efficient since the pump will be manual, but it will do."

"Let's get to it then," she said, excited to upgrade her home. "Come on."

Once dressed, she all but tore apart the cabin, looking for items they could use in the construction. There were many serviceable things, including some wire, cloths, old nails, and spikes. Remembering the rubber trees that grew along the riverbank, Kilani sprinted outside to gather some of the broad leaves, realizing they could use them as stoppers for the pump.

They toiled for hours, falling into conversation as they worked, and Alrec asked her about the previous owners.

"I have no idea," she said, carving a slit at the end of one of the bamboo stalks so she could attach it to another and bind them. "Kenden found the shed when he used to hunt and fish with his father before the Awakening. Whoever built it must've wanted to hide from the world too."

"I've heard rumors of other immortal species that exist besides the Vampyres, Slayers, and Deamons," Alrec said, smoothing one of the stalks with the sander he'd fashioned from a slab of tree bark. "Do you think it's possible?"

"Anything is possible," she said with a shrug. "I mean, humans exist beyond the ether and have some pretty crazy stories that have outlived their mortal bodies. Everyone is convinced they'll remain separate from us for eternity, but I have my doubts."

"Do you have a soft spot for humans then?"

"No," she said, wrinkling her nose. "They're still heathens. But we can learn a lot from their failures and wars, and their successes and triumphs. My brother always believed we would adopt their technology one day."

"Perhaps, but that day seems far away in an immortal world that clings to tradition."

"Truth," she muttered, snapping the bamboo pieces together.

They tinkered for another hour until they trailed outside to use the remaining hours of the night to spar. Once inside, they fell into bed and loved each other slowly and tenderly.

Kilani opened herself to him, thanking him with her body and soulful moans as he rained kisses upon her heated skin.

Chapter 17

Alrec continued to construct the plumbing system for Kilani, wondering when her excited smiles and heartfelt words of thanks had become the entire zenith of his existence. Every time she would gaze at him with those wide blue eyes, sparkling with gratitude, Alrec's heart would click further into place. It was as if the organ had never fully functioned until he met his stunning Slayer.

He dug a well behind the home, and using the bamboo pipes they'd molded, he managed to create a makeshift plumbing system for her over the next week. At night, they continued to spar, and Alrec knew he was pushing off the inevitable.

He was fully healed, and it was time for him to return home.

Although he was entranced by the woman who'd saved his life, Alrec had a duty, and he felt a calling to fulfill it. Such was the way when your people were at war, and even though he longed to stay with Kilani, honor and purpose ran deep.

After another long night of toiling with the plumbing system, Alrec placed the final touches on the manual pump, testing it out before declaring Kilani should give it a try. Under the light of the moon, she pumped the mechanism by the well, emitting a joyful cry when it worked and water gushed through the newly laid pipes to the house. Rushing inside, she turned the knob of the bamboo faucet he'd constructed over the basin. Water trickled into the sink, and she covered her mouth, exhilaration sparkling in her eyes as she jumped up and down.

"We did it," she cried before lowering her hands and shrugging. "Well, *you* really did it, but I helped where I could. I have running water. Never thought I'd see the day."

Taken by her genuine delight, he slid his palm over hers and squeezed. "I'm so thrilled it makes you happy," he said, his voice rough with emotion since he knew it was one of the last times he would gaze into her stunning eyes. "I like making you happy, Kilani."

"Alrec," she whispered, stepping closer and palming his cheeks, "you make me so happy. I would choose these weeks with you over an eternity with any other man. Thank you."

Sliding his arms around her waist, he drew her close, aligning their bodies as he gazed deep into her eyes. "Can't we figure out a way to make this work? To stay together even though it seems impossible?"

Compassion clouded her features as she caressed his jaw. "I don't see a way—"

"Would you consider coming to Astaria with me?"

Her mouth fell open as shock laced her expression. Sadness coursed through him as she slowly shook her head.

"You know I can't. Our people are at war, Alrec. I won't live my life under the rule of a species that hunts and drains my people for blood."

"We only abduct men, not women or children, and it's only because your blasted king is intent on extending the war. It's because of his ludicrous suicide decree we must hunt so often."

"I'm no fan of Marsias, but he does what he believes is just. Your people are not innocent, Alrec. How many Slayers have been abducted from their families and died in your dungeon?"

His eyebrows drew together as his mind raced to find a solution. "I would protect you —"

Laughter sprang from her throat as she covered his lips with her fingers. "Do you really think I'm the type of woman who will sit home and wait for a man to protect me?" Arching a brow, her lips curved into a sad smile. "I would hate that life. Plus, we could never bear children together. It's an eternity I would never push you into."

Forming a slight pout, he spoke against her fingers. "How can I accept this is the end? I'm not sure of much, little one, but I'm certain of one thing..." Resting his forehead against hers, he brushed a kiss on her lips. "I will never care for another woman the way I care for you. *Never.*"

Tears glistened in her eyes as her lips wobbled. "Nor I for you. Now, show me. Love me for the last time, so I can remember. And then, when dusk arrives tomorrow, you must begin the journey home. You can always hold the memory here too." Placing her palm over his heart, she squeezed. "We'll treasure them together even when we're apart."

Overcome with despair at the unfairness of the world, Alrec lowered and lifted her, clutching on for dear life as she wrapped her legs around his waist. Thrusting his fingers in her hair, he crashed their lips together, plunging deep inside, unable to control his desperate need. She moaned, writhing against him as he carried her to bed.

And then, he tore away their clothes, determined to imprint every single detail so they would never forget.

Chapter 18

Kilani clung to Alrec, intent on pushing away her heartache and sadness so she could lose herself in his fervent kisses and warm embrace one last time. Once he dragged off their clothes, he placed her on the bed, crawling over her, the movements slow and protective. Looming above her, he pressed his lips to hers and drew her into a smoldering, desperate kiss.

"Wait," she said, placing her palm on his chest.

Confusion crossed his expression as he pulled back. "Sweetheart?"

Grinning, she wiggled underneath him before sliding off the bed. Grasping his shoulders, she urged him to lie flat on his back as his eyebrows drew together. With a sultry glance, she sauntered over to the corner and picked up the ropes that lay on the small table. Trailing back over, she encircled his wrist and lifted it to the bedpost.

"I remember you saying you were into the bondage thing," she rasped, securing his wrist before trailing to the other side and securing the other one.

Alrec smiled and tugged on the ropes. "It seems we've come full circle."

A hoarse laugh bounded from her throat. "My dear Vampyre, you have no idea."

Sliding one leg over his massive frame, she straddled him, aware of the wetness that seeped from her deepest place onto his abdomen just above his hard shaft. He shimmied under her, his cock searching for her warmth, and she lifted a finger before shaking her head.

"No rushing," she commanded, leaning forward and brushing her lips against his. "We're going to take this one slow."

Alrec's eyes glazed with lust as his breathing grew heavy. "Do your worst, little one. I can't wait."

Her lips curled into a sexy grin as she slid up his body and touched her nipple to his lips. "Suck me, Vampyre—"

The words were abruptly cut off as she gasped when he drew the taut nub into his wet mouth. Kilani moaned, writhing above him as he lapped and licked the puckered bud. Staring into his deep brown orbs, she eventually withdrew from his tender ministrations and slid her other breast to his mouth, longing for more. Her sexy Vampyre gazed at her as he loved her, and Kilani realized she might be embroiled in the most erotic moment she would ever experience. Yearning to give him pleasure, she popped her breast from his mouth and began to trail kisses down his body.

The prickly hairs of his chest tickled her nose as she worked her way down, reveling in his hushed moans and the reverent way he breathed her name. Stopping at his navel, she dipped her tongue inside, pleased when he shivered in response.

"Sweetheart," he whispered, shaking his head on the pillow. "This is so sexy, but I want to touch you too."

"Soon," she murmured, her lips carving a path to the juncture between his thighs where his erection stood firm and proud. Resting on her knees, she cradled him in her hands, moisture gushing between her thighs as he groaned when she squeezed.

"You're *very* swollen here," she said, biting her lip as she began to work his flesh between her hands. "My poor, injured Vampyre."

"There's nothing injured in that area," he muttered, his body bowing atop the bed. "Goddess, Kilani...please...don't tease me..."

Lowering, she ran the tip of her nose over his sensitive flesh, closing her eyes to memorize the feel of his taut skin and musky scent. Extending her tongue, she ran it over the length once...twice...before staring deep in his eyes and lifting the engorged head to her lips.

"I'm honored to love you like this," she whispered against the quivering flesh, repeating the words he'd spoken the first night they'd made love.

"I'm honored to be loved by you...*my beautiful Kilani...*"

Connected with him through their gaze and deep-rooted emotion, she opened wide and slid over his throbbing cock. Alrec groaned, hips surging high on the bed as he uttered a curse. Determined to please him, she worked her wet mouth over the straining flesh, pumping the base with her hand as she lathered him with her tongue.

His passionate moans grew louder...deeper... and his shaft surged in her mouth, claiming every crevice as she gave herself to him, body and soul. Popping him from her lips, she ran her palm over the strained shaft, arching a brow as she silently asked him if she should continue.

"It feels so good, but I need to be inside you, little one," he rasped from above. "Please, untie me."

Taking pity on him, she snaked up his body, straddling his stomach and removing the binds. His hands flew to her hips, grasping firmly as he pushed her down his body. Sliding her wet core over his cock, he glided himself to her entrance. Kilani reached between them, aligning his tip to her center, and then she slowly enveloped him between her sensitive folds, overcome with the deep, full sensation.

"There you are," he whispered, hips jutting back and forth as he dragged himself through her taut channel. "So tight...so wet...made just for me..."

Kilani tossed her head back, whimpering at the possessive words.

"*My little Slayer.* Yes, that's it...keep riding me...goddess, you feel so good..."

She worked her hips tirelessly, undulating against him in the hope he would remember this moment centuries down the road, when they were both far removed from this place and time. Suddenly, his hands tightened on her hips, and he jolted forward, flipping them so she lay on her back as he loomed above her. Gazing into her, he threaded his fingers through the hair at her temple as his cock worked her quivering body.

"Kilani..." he whispered, love blazing in his deep orbs. "I have to tell you—"

"Don't," she interrupted, tears burning her eyes as she covered his lips with her fingers. "If you say it, I won't be able to let you go. Please, Alrec..."

With a ragged groan, he lowered his face to her neck, kissing the trembling skin as his cock thrust deep inside her. Encircling his broad shoulders, she dug her nails into his back and offered the last thing she had to give: "Drink from me."

His head snapped back, and his worried gaze studied hers. "Are you sure? I'll be able to read your thoughts and feelings—"

"I'm sure," she rasped, nodding on the pillow as their bodies vibrated with unsaid emotion. "The words are too much, but I need you to know."

Groaning her name, he lowered his lips to her neck, licking the soft flesh to coat it with his self-healing saliva and shield her from the pain. Kilani closed her eyes, her fingers clutching his flesh as the tips of his fangs scratched her delicate skin atop her pulsing vein. Bracing, her muscles tensed before he growled—sending jolts of desire through her heated body—and plunged his fangs into her neck.

Pleasure unlike anything she'd ever known coursed through her frame as blissful laughter leaped from her throat. Alrec's lips worked the flesh at her neck, sucking the life force from her vein as his thick cock dragged against every cell of her wet core. Clutching him to her ravaged body, stars exploded behind her eyes as his hips thrust at a furious pace. Screaming his name, her body arched beneath him, and she began to come, joy consuming every thought and every inch of her shuddering frame. Alrec moaned against her neck, and she knew his violent trembles meant he was close. Opening to him, she held nothing back, needing him to know how special he was to her...and would always be.

Her magnificent Vampyre lifted his head, eyes glazed with passion as he stared at her, lips red and swollen from her blood and their heated kisses. Pressing his forehead to hers, he growled low and deep in his chest, surging his fingers into her hair and latching tightly. Resting his cheek against hers, he came, shooting pulsing jets of release inside her, claiming her one last time.

Kilani held him, grateful to give him such pleasure...understanding he was *everything*. Her one true mate. Regardless of the fact a future between them was impossible, she would always carry him deep in her heart and acknowledge him as *hers*.

"Good grief, woman," he muttered, kissing a trail down her cheek to the puncture wounds on her neck. Extending his tongue, he began to slowly lick them closed, healing them with his saliva, and she reveled in the smooth, silken strokes.

Once the wounds were closed, they lay entwined, sweaty and sated, until he slowly rose to wet a cloth. Returning to the bed, his lips formed a lazy grin as he cleaned the evidence of their loving from between her thighs. After cleaning himself, he slid between the sheets, drawing her to his side.

Resting her cheek on his chest, she cursed the tears in her eyes, vowing not to let them fall. The conclusion of their affair had always been carved in stone, and she wouldn't allow sadness to pervade their last night together. Snuggling into him, she took comfort in the rise and fall of his chest as his breaths grew heavy.

"I feel the same," he murmured, kissing her hair as his hand softly stroked her back. "I need you to know, Kilani. It wouldn't be fair for me to know your feelings and you not to know mine in return."

Her heart slammed at his admission, knowing he didn't have to return the sentiment he'd absorbed through her blood: she loved him with her whole heart and always would.

"A Vampyre with a sense of fair play," she teased, unable to acknowledge the deeper feelings that clogged her throat. "Who knew those existed?"

His deep chuckle rumbled against her, and she closed her eyes, inhaling his heady scent. God, she would miss it when he was gone. There were so many things she would miss about the honorable man who'd spared her life so she could spare his in return.

"Sweet dreams, little one."

"Sweet dreams, Alrec."

Comforted by the silken caresses upon her back, Kilani clutched him close, fighting sleep since it brought her one step closer to his departure. As his warmth surrounded her, the emotion she'd held at bay tightened her throat to the point of pain. Unable to control it, she nuzzled into his hand when he swiped away the tear that trailed down her cheek.

"Shhh..." he soothed, kissing her forehead. "I know, sweetheart."

Somewhere between dawn and dusk she eventually slept, knowing she would have to rise with the moon and tell her Vampyre goodbye.

Chapter 19

Alrec rose at dusk, a sense of melancholy dragging every bone and muscle in his body as he dressed. Kilani watched him from the bed, her eyes sad and morose, before she rose and tugged on her clothing.

Kilani packed a bag for him filled with three containers of her blood, a small knife, and some cloths he could use to bathe with when he reached the River Thayne. Stepping outside, she trailed to the back of the home and located her finest spear. Returning, she offered it to him, arms outstretched, and he smiled.

"I thought you enjoyed stabbing fish with that one the most. Or perhaps stabbing me when we sparred."

Breathing a laugh, she nodded. "It's definitely my favorite. Take it and use it to fight any Deamons who get in your way. I don't like their chances against you with my spear."

Alrec took it, sliding it through a loop on the bag now secured to his back. Stepping forward, he cupped her face, sliding his thumb over her lips as her eyes shone in the moonlight.

"Thank you for saving my life, little one. I'll never forget your kindness."

"Well, you saved mine first," she said, lifting a shoulder, "so we're even. Can't be indebted to a Vampyre. Told you that from the beginning."

His eyes roved over her face, memorizing every freckle and dimple as he recalled the rush of feeling he'd experienced when he drank from her only hours ago. Her love for him was pure and true, and he returned the sentiment a thousand times over. It didn't matter they'd had only weeks in the cabin; he'd begun his descent into love with her in a meadow under a full moon five years ago, and their time together had only exacerbated the emotion. Doubt crept into his slowly breaking heart, and he wondered if he was truly making the right choice.

"It's the only way," she whispered, lifting to her toes and pressing a kiss to his lips. "We both know it. Travel safely, Alrec. Be kind to my people. Perhaps one day, centuries from now, I'll see you again when we're at peace and the world has evolved to embrace me. It's my greatest wish."

"I think you're magnificent," he rasped, leaning down to give her a blazing kiss. "I accept you exactly as you are, Kilani."

Nodding, she stepped back, breaking their embrace since he didn't have the strength to. Lifting her hand, she gave a slight wave. "Give 'em hell."

Alrec's throat bobbed, so clogged with emotion he could barely breathe. Returning her wave, he flashed one last somber, poignant smile. And then, he slowly turned and left the woman who owned his heart.

It took Alrec weeks to navigate back to Astaria. At night, he would travel across the grueling landscape, making the most of the darkness to find his way home. During the day, he would find a heavily covered area or cave to sleep in to shield himself from the sun. He was always cognizant that Deamons could be lurking in unseen alcoves and remained on high alert.

Fortunately, he only ran into one Deamon cluster. It was a group of five Deamons that began trailing him as he approached the River Thayne from the foothills of the Strok Mountains. They were sloppy and quite easily observed by his honed skills, so he continued forward until the glow of dusk began to paint the horizon. Locating a dense thicket of trees, he pretended to set up camp as the Deamons surrounded him. Grasping his spear, which lay hidden on the ground, Alrec whirled and began to fight the creatures, thankful for his sparring sessions with Kilani. They had certainly increased his stamina, and training with someone so skilled only enhanced his abilities.

Eventually, four Deamons lay dead on the ground, and Alrec fought the last one, besting him after several minutes and thrusting the spear between his eyes. The creature died instantly, confirming Kilani's intel. Pleased, Alrec vowed to speak to Latimus as soon as he returned. The commander would want to know about the weakness, and his younger brother, Heden, was a genius at creating new weapons to maim their enemies. Perhaps he could create a device designed to injure the Deamons in their vulnerable spot.

When he eventually crested the hill that led to Astaria, Alrec trekked across the meadow to the imposing Vampyre compound, expecting to be thrilled he'd made it home alive. Instead, he felt rather numb as he approached the outer wall. Stopping outside the thick stones, he lifted his hand to his mouth and shouted.

"Hello? Is anyone guarding the wall? It's Alrec, son of Jakar."

"Alrec?" a deep voice called. "We don't have a lot of men stationed here due to the protective shield Etherya placed on the wall, but I hear you! It's Takel. Give me a moment."

Stepping back, Alrec waited until the stones began to slide open. Walking inside, he noticed the soldiers pushing the door closed as Takel approached and patted him on the back.

"My god, Alrec. We thought you were dead! I sent a search party out for two weeks, but we never found you."

"I ended up floating several miles downriver," Alrec said, cupping the man's shoulder with genuine affection. "It's an unbelievable story and one I can't wait to tell you. For now, I'm exhausted and need my warm bed."

"Fair enough, my friend. Commander Latimus will want to hear your story, I'm sure. I'll set up a debrief tomorrow night."

Following his friend, Alrec headed farther into the compound before striding down the dirt road that led to his cabin near the far wall. Once inside, he inhaled a deep breath, hoping he would gain comfort from the familiar surroundings. Instead, as he unloaded his pack and stashed the remaining container of

Kilani's blood in the ice box, all he felt was loneliness.

Chapter 20

Alrec threw himself back into fighting, assuming that if he performed the duty he was born to fulfill, the loneliness would soon abate. After all, he'd lived alone for centuries before the Awakening, and when his family died in the tragic event, his solitude had only grown. Although he missed his parents terribly, he'd made his peace with their deaths and vowed to avenge them. That vow had always been enough.

Until *her*.

Now, Alrec ached with a yearning so vast he sometimes wondered if he was slowly going insane. Kilani's image had flashed through his mind with fair regularity ever since he met her on the Slayer meadow. But after their time in the cabin, where she'd graciously saved his life and welcomed him into her embrace, he was fairly sure he was addicted to her melodious laughter and tender soul.

Was it possible to be addicted to another immortal? If so, what did it mean for his future? Alrec took his duty as a soldier seriously and didn't want his skills to become compromised because he was distracted by thoughts of a fierce Slayer with gorgeous blue eyes...

The first few weeks he returned home, he found himself listlessly wandering throughout his tiny home. Dazed and unfocused, he constantly knocked his shin against the chest at the base of his bed or banged his elbow on his bathroom doorknob. Even though he healed quickly, the clumsiness was a nuisance he could only attribute to his fixation on the woman he missed so vehemently.

Sometimes, when he rapped his knee against the bedpost, Alrec's hand reflexively stretched to stroke the wood. Lost in memories, he remembered how Kilani bound his ankles to her bed before he earned her trust. Caressing the wood, he would recall her upturned face in the moonlight the night she finally kissed him. Then he realized he was stroking a goddamn bedpost and told himself to get a grip.

A month after his return, Latimus ordered a raid on Uteria. Alrec did his duty, abducting three Slayer men as he cursed the war and hatred between the species. If things were different, perhaps he and Kilani could build a life together. Although the species had never intermarried before the Awakening, the kingdom was vastly in need of change, and loving a member of the opposite species would certainly mean progress to some.

But Alrec was smart enough to know deep-rooted change took time—most likely centuries—so he carried out his duty, understanding there was no guarantee he or Kilani would survive long enough to see such progress. It was just the way of their war-torn world.

Every day at dawn, Alrec reentered his cabin, situated in a cul-de-sac filled with other laborers and soldiers' dwellings on the outskirts of Astaria. After completing the mundane task of filling his goblet with Slayer blood, he winced at the bitter taste. Now that he'd tasted Kilani's rich blood on his tongue, the life force of a Slayer soldier was a stale, tasteless substitute. Longing for her, he lolled on his bed each morning, lightly clutching the sheets, wishing it was her soft hair or silken skin.

After several months of existing in his listless state, Alrec admitted his existence was becoming quite pointless. Unfortunately, there was no resolution to his predicament in the foreseeable future.

One night, three months after he returned home, Alrec was sparring on the training field alongside his battalion. Takel rushed him, sword held high, and Alrec took a sloppy swipe, attempting to knock his weapon free. Takel laughed and knocked Alrec's weapon from his hand, glaring down at him as Alrec took a knee.

"By the goddess, Alrec," he said, nicking his neck with the sword and spurring a reflexive, angry growl from Alrec's throat. "What happened to you? You can't fight worth shit anymore. You never used to yield. I'm worried."

"That's enough," Commander Latimus's deep voice boomed behind them. "Sheathe your sword, Takel. Alrec, I'd like to speak to you privately."

Sighing, Alrec took Takel's offered hand and rose before silently stalking up the hill behind Latimus. Once they stood side by side, Latimus crossed his arms over his chest and kicked the grass with the toe of his boot.

"This can't go on, Alrec," he said softly. "Your mind is elsewhere, and I have no need for a soldier who can't fight."

Expelling a breath, Alrec glanced at the ground as shame washed over him. "My one duty is to avenge my family as a soldier, and I am failing. I'm sorry, Commander."

Latimus's jaw ticked in the silver moonlight. "You told us of the intel you gathered while you were gone. You said you learned it when you killed some Deamons on your journey."

Nodding, Alrec acknowledged the white lie. He hadn't told anyone about meeting Kilani because he didn't want to jeopardize her safety or tell her secrets. Instead, he told everyone he'd washed down the river and found the cabin when he regained consciousness. Then he nursed himself back to health and traveled home.

"Your story technically makes sense, but I find myself wondering how you stayed alive without consuming Slayer blood."

Alrec pursed his lips. Latimus was shrewd, and the question was valid. "As I told you, I found a barrel full of blood near the cabin. It must have been left there from the blood-bankings before the Awakening."

Latimus breathed a laugh before harshly rubbing his forehead. "You know, you're a terrible liar, Alrec. Probably because you're an honorable man who lies infrequently."

Alrec pursed his lips. "Perhaps."

Wide nostrils flared as Latimus inhaled a deep breath. "If there's one thing I recognize on a man, it's the look of being in love with a woman he can't have."

His gaze whipped to Latimus as he studied his stern expression. "Don't tell me you're in love with someone you can't have. You're the most powerful soldier in the realm and brother to King Sathan. You can have any woman you choose."

Scoffing, Latimus kicked the ground. "I'm a bastard who doesn't know the first thing about loving a woman I'll never deserve."

"Who is she? Perhaps I can help—"

"It's not meant to be," Latimus interjected, his tone firm. "And I urge you to never speak of it again." Facing him, Latimus's ice-blue eyes drilled into his. "But my situation is not yours, Alrec. I don't want you to live in misery as I do. At least one of us should be happy."

Feeling his eyebrows draw together, he pondered. "I won't shirk my duty. And I wouldn't be a man worthy of her if I did."

Placing his hands on his hips, Latimus studied the ground, appearing deep in thought. Finally, his gaze lifted, and he spoke with resolution. "I've been wanting to create a new position in the army for a while, but it's daunting and requires much sacrifice. There's never been anyone I could see filling it."

Slightly confused, Alrec swallowed. "Okay."

"The soldier would have to leave Astaria behind and live a solitary life near the Deamon caves. Essentially, I want a full-time scout to keep a constant eye on the growing Deamon threat. The soldier would have to surveil the area, gather intel, and travel back to Astaria every six months to give me a report."

Alrec worked his mouth, trying to form a response. Was Latimus offering him a chance to return to Kilani and continue to fulfill his duty to the army?

"It's not an easy assignment. The soldier won't be able to see his family at Astaria except when he returns to gather supplies and report to me. Since you don't have any family here, I anticipate that won't be a problem."

"No, sir."

"I'll expect detailed reports and trust you to work autonomously. This is not a vacation, Alrec. It's an important role I need filled. There are very few soldiers I would even consider assigning." Cupping his shoulder, he squeezed. "*You* are one of those soldiers. Know this assignment will require you to live near the Deamon caves until we have eradicated Crimeous and the Deamon threat. It could be centuries."

Rising to his full height, Alrec saluted his commander as blood pulsed through his body. "I understand and accept your assignment, sir."

Chuckling, Latimus arched a brow. "You didn't hesitate. Holy shit. You've got it bad, my friend."

Grinning, Alrec shrugged. "I don't want to divulge her secret, but since you're trusting me..." Leaning forward, he whispered, "Sir, I can't explain it. I've never felt this way before. It's...*consuming*. She's taken residence in my head and my heart, and I can't escape her."

"If she is a Slayer, you will never be able to bear children," Latimus said softly.

"No." Alrec ran the sole of his boot over the grass. "I can't speak for her, but that doesn't bother me. In a world as consumed with war as ours, there are always children that need parents. If we decided to choose that path in the future, I would be honored to adopt a child with her."

"I don't want to pry, but if she lives separate from her people, as I assume since you told me the cabin was far from Uteria, her only option to adopt a child would be to take in a Vampyre. Would she be open to raising a child who is not her own species?"

Glancing toward the horizon, Alrec debated the question. "Well, she saved me, so I guess saving another Vampyre or two wouldn't be out of the question." He held up his hands, showing his palms. "I wouldn't want to speak for her though. She's tough as nails. It would have to be a decision we make together."

"If she's that tough, you'd be smart to have her accompany you on your scouting missions."

"Sir," Alrec said with a deep smile, "I wouldn't have it any other way."

Chuckling, Latimus nodded. "Then it's settled. How much time do you need to wrap things up here?"

"I'll sell my cabin as quickly as possible, and I'd like to say a proper goodbye to Takel and the other men before I leave. Otherwise, I can probably begin the post in a month."

Placing his hand on his hip, Latimus's lips curved into a genuine smile, which was rarely seen from the gruff, stoic commander. "You're a good man, Alrec. Be happy. You deserve it. Come see me before you leave, and we'll choose a date for you to return home and give me your first report." With a salute, he began walking down the hill.

"Latimus!"

Pivoting, he called, "Yes?"

"You deserve to be happy too."

A moment passed before he softly replied, "It's not in the cards for me, my friend, but I'm certainly thrilled for you. Go seize it for both of us. See ya."

Alrec watched his broad shoulders as he strode away, feeling a strange sense of comradery for the strong, enduring commander. Gazing toward the sky, he uttered, "Thank you, Etherya." Closing his eyes, he imagined returning home to Kilani, hoping she would welcome him as her mate and partner...for as long as they both shall live...

Knowing there was only one way to find out, Alrec trekked down the hill, ready to tie up his affairs at Astaria so he could return to his little one.

Chapter 21

Kilani's mood progressively devolved from bad to worse to catastrophic with each day that passed after Alrec's departure. Of course, she'd known it would take some time to get over him—after all, how many times did you meet the love of your damn life? Only once, if the soothsayers' tales rang true—and deep in her heart, Kilani knew Alrec was her soul mate.

Since having a Vampyre as a soul mate was a futile endeavor, she tightened her bootstraps and pushed through each day, determined to make a life for herself in the place she'd chosen. The first task she set out to accomplish was revising her sleep schedule so she slept at night again like a normal damn person. Intent on retraining herself, she lay down in the lonely bed each night only to feel her eyes well with emotion that her lover wasn't by her side. Most nights, she would rise and walk along the river, remembering the spots that held such meaning for her.

The clearing by the old oak tree where Alrec first held her and pressed those broad, firm lips to hers under the twinkling stars.

The grassy knoll where they'd sparred, strengthening his muscles so he would survive the journey home.

The soft grass where he'd gently urged her down and eased away her clothes...as calmly and steadily as he'd eased her reservations about loving a Vampyre. Trailing to the spot, Kilani lowered and crossed her legs before running her palm over the grass. It tickled her skin, reminding her of Alrec's prickly hairs when she'd caressed his chiseled chest.

Sighing, Kilani stared at the stars and cursed every god she didn't believe in for sending her the perfect companion only to rip him away when she'd finally given every last piece of her soul.

"I know we disowned you after the Awakening," she murmured, addressing Etherya although she knew the goddess cared naught for Slayers anymore. Not since her species had devolved into war, breaking the goddess's heart until she withdrew her protection. "But you could throw me a bone, you know?" Kilani continued, sitting back and resting her palms flat on the grass. "You're a badass woman too, right? Female goddesses are way cooler than men. You see the logic in letting me win at *something*, right?"

Silence was her only answer as the soft breeze flitted through the treetops.

Suddenly, a branch snapped in the distance, and Kilani lurched to her feet, crouching in a defensive stance as she perked her ears. Was it a Deamon? Had they finally discovered her cabin? Of course they wouldn't discover it when a hulking Vampyre soldier was in residence.

"That would be too much good fortune for your unlucky ass, Kilani," she muttered, rising and stalking toward the sound. Eyes wide, she picked up a branch, pleased when she noticed its sharp edge. If the bastards were going to kill her, she'd at least go down fighting.

"This is my home, and you're trespassing," she said, frustrated at the slight waver in her voice. "I'm prepared to defend it till my dying breath."

A soft whimper echoed between the trees, causing the hairs on her nape to rise. Slowly walking forward, she passed a row of ferns to see a white wolf standing in the clearing. His sky-blue gaze locked onto hers, and she realized he was as terrified as she was.

"Whoa," she said, showing him her palm as she gingerly approached. "I'm not going to hurt you. Where's your pack?"

The wolf uttered a soft, high-pitched wail and looked off into the distance before reclaiming her gaze.

"They left you, huh?" Inching closer, she assessed his mangy ears and the gray fur along his back that swirled with the white. "From your size, I assume you're the runt. You're big, but not as big as some wolves I've seen around here. Believe me, I get it. Sometimes, you just don't fit in."

The wolf harrumphed before lowering to the ground. Tilting his head, he began to pant, his long pink tongue shining under the moonlit clouds.

"Oh no," she said, holding up her hands and backing away. "I'm not in the market for a pet. Don't look all cute. It's not happening." Gesturing with the stick, she urged him to run along. "Go on, now. Some rabbits live in the bushes over there. I'm sure they'll make a fine dinner."

Turning, she trekked back to the house, noting the branches and leaves that crunched behind her. Frustrated the animal was following her, she roughly closed the door and attempted to sleep.

The next night, consumed with thoughts of Alrec, she headed out for a walk since sleeping was futile. As she crested the bank of the river, the wolf was waiting for her as if he knew she would appear.

"Nope," she said, shaking her head as she pointed to the far-off mountains. "Not happening. I don't want a mangy mongrel around here. Got it?" Stomping down the riverbank, she repeated the mantra in her mind that she was *not* adopting a pet.

The nightly walks continued, and eventually, Kilani became used to the sightings of her furry friend. They were a welcome distraction from her obsession with Alrec and gave her something else to focus on.

A few weeks after first seeing the wolf, she decided to bring it some dinner.

"Here," she said, tossing him one of the fish she'd cooked for dinner. "I even cooked it for you, you lucky bastard."

The wolf uttered a series of excited yelps before resting on his laurels and devouring the fish.

After a few weeks and much deliberation, Kilani accepted she was going to adopt the damn mutt. The last thing she needed was another mouth to feed, but loneliness was slowly eating her away as it pervaded her soul, and the only person who could fix that was never coming back. So, she grabbed a rope one warm, balmy night and headed to the river, intent on laying down the ground rules.

"You're going to do your part around here," she said, sliding the rope around the wolf's neck as she patted his soft fur. "And we're going to take lots of baths in the river. I won't have fleas in my home, do you hear me?"

The wolf chortled, panting with obvious affection, and Kilani led him home with the makeshift leash. Once there, she filled a basin with water and brought it outside before scrubbing the creature so thoroughly she thought his fur might molt. He rang himself dry, spraying droplets of water across the yard, and Kilani experienced her first moment of joy since Alrec's departure.

"Good boy," she said, petting his wet fur as she sat beside him. "Wait...you're a boy, right?" Peeking, she confirmed with a nod. "Yep, a boy. Now, what are we going to call you?"

The mongrel just stared at her before craning his head and uttering a high-pitched sound.

"Well, you're more a dog than a wolf, aren't you?" Standing, she scratched behind his ears. "I'll think of something. In the meantime, come on inside. I'm going to dry you off, and you're going to cuddle with me. You're going to be a poor substitute, but you'll have to do."

His paws echoed on her wooden floor as she brought him inside and toweled him dry. After crawling into bed, she patted the covers, and he jumped in with her, barking before shimmying against her legs atop the sheets.

"I miss him so much," she whispered, slowly stroking the wolf's head. "Will it always hurt like this?"

Her new friend only whimpered before placing his chin on her thigh and closing his eyes. Sighing, Kilani blew out the candle and did the same.

Chapter 22

A few weeks later, Kilani finally began sleeping at night. Although she wasn't sleeping through the *entire* night, there were times when her brain allowed her to let go of her yearning and recharge. Having a warm body next to her was comforting, and she cherished her new companion even though she inwardly chided herself for capitulating so quickly. Perhaps Alrec had softened her. Regardless, she loved the little bugger and was extremely thankful for his presence in her small home.

One night, she was jolted from a deep sleep by the wolf's low growl. Swiping her hair from her face, she rose and pointed at his nose.

"Don't bark, okay? I'm going to go look around, and I'll leave the door cracked. If I need you, I'll call you, but otherwise, stay inside."

The wolf whimpered.

"I don't want you to get hurt." Placing a kiss between his ears, she grabbed the spear by the door placed her hand on the knob. Inhaling a deep breath, she slowly pulled it open.

Broad shoulders trekked toward her, illuminated by the full moon, and Kilani's breath caught in her throat. Stepping onto the soft grass, she whispered, "Alrec?"

His large frame continued to advance, and she rubbed her eyes, telling herself she was still asleep and dreaming. Holding up her hand, she shook her head. "No."

He froze, his features unreadable in the dim light as her chin slightly wobbled. "Don't come any closer. Please..."

Lifting his hand to the back of his neck, he massaged the weary muscles. "Uh...I was rather hoping for a more receptive greeting."

Shocked laughter exited her throat as she shook her head. "This is a dream, Kilani. You're going to wake up and it will be morning..."

"Sweetheart," he called, sliding the pack from his shoulders and dropping it to the ground before continuing to walk forward... one tentative step...then another... "It's me. You're not dreaming."

"Don't give me hope," she rasped, closing her eyes as she tried to discern reality from the surreal. "I just learned how to function without hope...I can't go back..." Lifting her lids, his handsome features came into focus as he stopped several feet away.

Lowering to one knee, he extended his hand and beckoned to her. "I learned to live that way too, but it was no way to live, little one. We deserve better. We deserve *more*. Let me give it to you." He shook his hand, and Kilani felt her heart swell with love.

"Alrec," she whispered, taking a hesitant step forward. "You came back to me?"

"I came back to you," he said with a nod. "Come on, little one. I don't want to live one more moment without touching you." Extending his fingers, he smiled. "Goddess, I missed you."

A strangled cry left her lips as she threw down the spear and broke into a full-on sprint. Alrec's deep laughter echoed off the trees as she bolted into his arms, knocking the wind out of him as they both tumbled to the ground. Straddling him as his back splayed over the grass, she rained ardent kisses over every inch of his face.

"Oh my god," she breathed in between the heated kisses. "I never thought I'd see you again. How did you...? Where did you...? Why did you...?"

Chuckling, he thrust his fingers in her hair, lifting her head so he could smile into her eyes. "There's time for that, little one. Let's just say I was miserable without you—and a pretty terrible soldier—so Latimus secured another position for me."

"Another position? Out here?"

"Out here, Kilani. In the home where we fell in love and where we'll create our future. If you'll have me." Embracing her, he rose to sit on the grass, and she wrapped her legs around his waist, determined to hold on for dear life so he'd never leave again.

"I'll have you," she murmured, resting her forehead to his and brushing a kiss over his broad lips. "But will you have me? I feel like you're sacrificing so much to live with me in a secluded cabin in the woods—"

His lips consumed hers, cutting off the words as she groaned with desire. Opening, she let him plunder her, sliding her tongue over his in return, reveling in his taste. His tongue swept every crevice of her mouth before he pulled back to place a trail of soft kisses over her bottom lip.

"I can't live without you, little one," he murmured, the words vibrating against her swollen lips. "You're stuck with me. But we're going to have to expand the house and improve the plumbing. Thankfully, I can restock on supplies when I return to Astaria."

Her pounding heart turned to stone in her chest. "When you return?"

"Once every six months, sweetheart. That's all. Otherwise, I'm yours for eternity."

"Alrec..." Stroking his face, her eyes darted over his austere features, deep brown eyes, and the sexy growth of stubble along his jaw. "My very own Vampyre. Perhaps I *did* do something right in my godforsaken life after all."

Tossing back his head, he broke into a blissful laugh. "Perhaps you did, sweetheart." Running his hand over her hair, affection swam in his eyes.

A bark sounded behind them, and Alrec arched a brow, craning his neck to look at the wolf.

"I...uh..." Clearing her throat, she shrugged. "I adopted a wolf. He was the runt and abandoned by his pack. It seemed fitting."

Eyes sparkling with mirth, he asked, "What's his name?"

Kilani bit her lip. "Dog."

Laughing, Alrec shook his head. "Creative."

"Hey, it was the best I could come up with since I was stuck here in this lonely cabin with a broken heart."

Reverently gazing at her, Alrec drew the pad of his finger across her jaw. "I thought you never got lonely."

"Not until I fell in love with a Vampyre with a fantastic ass who installed mediocre plumbing. It was all downhill after that."

Narrowing his eyes, he planted his hand on the ground and pushed to his feet, holding her tight as her legs clung to his waist. "Mediocre plumbing, huh?" he teased, nipping her nose as he strode toward the house. "I'll show you mediocre, woman. I'm going to install the best damn system you've ever seen."

Sighing, she rested her cheek against his chest, inhaling his scent as he carried her inside. "So romantic. And if you do it naked, I'll be even happier."

Alrec's laughter bounded through the home as he tried to close the door. Dog uttered some high-pitched cries, and Kilani peered over Alrec's shoulder.

"You've got to stay outside for now, boy. My Vampyre's going to give me some hot, sexy lovin'. We'll let you in after."

"The dog is *not* sleeping on our bed," he muttered, closing the door as Dog whimpered outside.

"Um, yeah, I said that too, but he grows on you like a bad fungus. Trust me, he's going to end up sleeping with us."

Striding to the bed, Alrec lowered her before sliding over her and aligning their bodies. "Honestly, sweetheart, I just don't care right now." Cementing his lips to hers, he thrust his tongue inside her mouth, drawing her into a dizzying kiss.

They tore at their clothes, tossing them aside until all that remained was their unsated lust and unwavering adoration. Staring deep into her eyes, Alrec cupped her shoulders, anchoring her as his shaft searched for her wet core. Gliding the tip of his cock through her slickness, he began to press inside. Kilani's swollen lips fell open in a silent cry, so thankful to have him home.

"I love you," she whispered, arching to meet his careful thrusts.

"I love you, little one."

Undulating his firm hips, her magnificent Vampyre took her to the edge of ecstasy and beyond as she accepted she would spend the rest of eternity with her soul mate after all.

And once they were sated and spent, Kilani padded to the door and let Dog inside...where he promptly carved out a spot at the foot of their entwined legs and fell asleep.

For Kilani, the possibility of the future they would build was brighter than any she could've imagined all those desolate years ago at Uteria. She'd had the strength to make a choice one night after a hard-fought battle, and the Universe had rewarded her with more than she'd ever dreamed.

It was the first of many happy endings upon Etherya's Earth.

Epilogue

T wo weeks after Alrec's return, he held Kilani's hand as they strolled toward the river. Dog trotted by their side, tongue lolling from his mouth as he panted. When they reached the spot where they'd shared their first kiss, Alrec drew to a stop and pulled her close.

"Ready, little one?"

Her vibrant beam all but melted his heart. "Ready."

Staring into each other's eyes, they repeated vows written long ago—some by Slayer soothsayers, some by Vampyre archivists—all meaningful to the two immortals who spoke them so reverently. After promising to love and cherish each other, they spoke the final declarations.

"I, Alrec, take you as my bonded mate, for all eternity."

"I, Kilani, take you as my husband for as long as we shall inhabit the realm."

Although each species had different terms for mates—"bonded" for Vampyres, and the more traditional "husband" and "wife" for Slayers—they each expressed the same sentiment. The promises were solemn commitments to be honored with care.

Leaning down, Alrec kissed his bonded mate, sealing their vows as Dog barked beside them. Giggling, she broke the kiss to tell the dog to hush before rising to her toes and drawing Alrec into another tender kiss.

"I swear, he really is a sweetheart. You're going to fall in love with him. Trust me."

Chuckling, Alrec pecked her lips before threading their fingers and squeezing. "We'll see." They resumed strolling along the river as he prepared himself to bring up the topic weighing on his mind. "You know, raising a dog is good practice for having a child."

Her eyes sparkled as she grinned up at him. "Is that so?"

"Mm-hmm." Their hands swung between them as he pondered how far to push. "I'd like to have one with you, sweetheart...if you're open to it. Latimus could help us adopt whenever we decide to take that step."

"A Vampyre child," she murmured, eyes narrowing. "I never imagined that for myself."

Disappointment coursed through him before her lips curved. "But I never imagined falling madly in love with a Vampyre, and that's turned out pretty well, so I'm definitely open."

"Yeah?"

"Yeah," she said with a nod. "Let's settle in here for a few decades and let you get comfortable with the new assignment. I'm *obviously* going to accompany you on your scouting missions. It's the perfect opportunity to use my skills, and I can protect you since I'm the superior warrior between us."

"Obviously," he droned, rolling his eyes.

She snickered as he winked.

"I still have no desire to help Vampyres, but I have a desire to help *you*, so I see the benefit. Deamons are a threat to Slayers too, and if I can help defeat them, even at the hands of Vampyres, I'll do it."

"I'm honored to have you by my side," he said, drawing her close and placing a kiss on her hair. "We make a formidable team."

"That we do. And once we're settled, I'd love to adopt a child with you, Alrec." Halting, she faced him and rose to her toes. "We're going to have a family. It's more than I thought I'd ever have. Thank you."

Embracing her, he allowed himself another kiss before they both turned to face the river.

Drawing her into his side, he rested his cheek against her temple as they gazed at the gurgling water. Dog sat beside them, nuzzling Kilani's leg as she burrowed into his embrace, and Alrec felt a moment of vivid harmony.

Their lives together had truly begun.

Dog's place at Kilani's side during their nightly walks remained constant until he grew old and crossed the Rainbow Bridge into the Passage.

And until Kilani adopted another stray a year later. And another after her.

Such became their pattern as they settled into their new lives.

Until the day they adopted their son, and he became best friends with each new pet they welcomed into their quaint, loving home.

Alrec and his Slayer had so many milestones to accomplish, and he couldn't wait to conquer every single one with Kilani as his partner and one true mate.

The goddess Etherya floated behind the dense thicket of trees, her white robes billowing in the soft wind as she observed the Vampyre soldier and the Slayer aristocrat. Never in her vast wisdom did she believe it possible two immortals from her now war-ravaged species would navigate their way to love so quickly. It was a much-needed omen of hope in a world that had devolved into evil and chaos.

Encouraged by the obvious affection shared between the two souls, Etherya closed her eyes and transported back to the Passage. She would clutch onto their affection as a beacon of faith and focus all her energy on manifesting reconciliation between Slayer Princess Miranda and Vampyre King Sathan.

The current state of war in their kingdoms resulted from the actions of previous generations, and perhaps the new rulers could be the ones to repair the damage. Only time would tell, and one thing Etherya possessed in her infinite providence was great patience.

So, she sat by the magnificent fountain in the misty, magical realm beyond her Earth and plotted...and waited...eager to observe— sometime in the not so distant future—the end of hatred between her beloved species.

Before You Go

Thank you so much for reading **The Dawn of Peace**! I've always wanted to write a prequel to this series and I hope you loved Kilani and Alrec as much as I did. Speaking of: would you like to read an *extra bonus epilogue* where you can meet their son? I wrote one for my newsletter subscribers. Just follow the link below to sign up for my newsletter and *you can download the bonus epilogue right away*. Happy reading!

Bonus Epilogue Download Link:
https://BookHip.com/XGZWPKL

Ready to see if Princess Miranda and King Sathan can reunite the species? Find out in **The End of Hatred**, available in eBook, Audio and Paperback!

If you have a moment to leave a review for this book on your retailer's site, BookBub, Goodreads, or anywhere else you review, this indie author would be eternally grateful. Thank you!

About the Author

USA Today bestselling author Rebecca Hefner grew up in Western NC and now calls the Hudson River of NYC home. In her youth, she would sneak into her mother's bedroom and read the romance novels stashed on the bookshelf, cementing her love of HEAs. A huge Buffy and Star Wars fan, she loves an epic fantasy and a surprise twist (Luke, he IS your father).

Before becoming an author, Rebecca had a successful twelve-year medical device sales career. After launching her own indie publishing company, she is now a full-time author who loves writing strong, complex characters who find their HEAs.

Rebecca can usually be found making dorky and/or embarrassing posts on TikTok and Instagram. Please join her so you can laugh along with her!

ALSO BY REBECCA HEFNER

Prevent the Past Series

Book 1: A Paradox of Fates
Book 2: A Destiny Reborn
Book 3: A Timeline Restored

The Etherya's Earth Series

Prequel: The Dawn of Peace
Book 1: The End of Hatred
Book 2: The Elusive Sun
Book 3: The Darkness Within
Book 4: The Reluctant Savior
Book 4.5: Immortal Beginnings
Book 5: The Impassioned Choice
Book 5.5: Two Souls United
Book 6: The Cryptic Prophecy
Book 6.5: Garridan's Mate
Book 7: Coming soon!